# Between These Caramel Thighs

# Acknowledgements

I would like to thank God for granting me the gift and ability to make others feel something. I would also like to thank my family and friends too as well; to name them all would be a most impossible feat. Thanks for being patient with me and pushing me to keep at it, no matter the obstacles that were thrown in my path. There are no words to describe how much your support has meant to me.

I wish to give thanks to Ms. Mckenney for her expertise at doing such a fine job at editing Between These Caramel Thighs. Thanks for putting up with my last minute changes and details, you are a gem!

I wish to give thanks to Mr. Hudson for the wonderful illustrations that he provided for Between These Caramel Thighs. Thanks for enhancing my stories with your visions of lustful delights!

I wish to give thanks to Mr. Jackson and Mr. Banks for doing such a fine job at promoting my book in cyberspace. Thanks so much!

Last, but not least, I would like to thank all of the men in the world who came alive once pen became intimate with paper.

### The Ramblings of a Lady in Heat awaiting the Taste of a Most Forbidden Treat!

He invades my sleep, disturbs my dreams, I want him so bad I could scream.

I long for the freedom to touch him

I am tortured every time I am near him

I want to press my lips against his, to taste him

I want to inhale him, his own special scent

I want to lick him, his skin, chest, and then his ass

I want to suck him, deep, deep

I want to drink from him, all of him

His mouth, his cock

Kiss him until I cannot breathe and then have him come inside of me, deep, so very deep

I want for him to ride me hard and leave his mark on my body…...my breasts, my nipples and between my ample thighs, my clit

### Secrets of a Lady

A page from the journal of a lady...

The shock of fur between my ample thighs enclose a sweet surprise

Come inside if you dare, step into this golden lair

Dream a dream of a summer's end

Tell me, my love, when will I see you once again

Folds slick with just a hint of dew

Come hold me, my love, I cannot wait to once again lie with you

Bodies intertwined in sweet sublime

Together, let us turn back the hands of time

Our bodies gleaming with a lover's passion

I pray to the God's above, let not the morning come and end our midnight session

For within these lines lie the secrets of a lady

## Take Me, take me once Again against the Wall

Bent over at the waist, her upper body resting against the wall, her hands rested on her ankles, she felt a fresh rush of blood run to her head. Dressed in a blush colored bra, a short jean skirt and white tube socks, she was in the process of getting fucked out of her mind. Breathing raggedly, she lifted up on her toes each time he thrust hard into her from behind. His hands gripping her hips, held her immobile as he thrust himself between the soft round moons of her caramel butt.

"I am going to give it to you, all of it," He said as he pulled almost out of her, then thrust back deep into her, making her go up on her toes, her legs slightly trembling.

"Is this what you want? My cock is so hard and it loves your wet warm pussy." He told her, and then he said, do you want me to cum inside of you and fill you up?"

"Yes, she said, gasping, I want this, do whatever you want, fill me, cum inside me." Hair and body wet with sweat, as her small pussy struggled to adjust to his size, girth and length.

"I am going to cum, he said a few minutes later, and I want for you to take it, take all of it." His hips slammed into hers once more and then he went still as sperm warm from his body shot into her dripping wetness.

A second later, he pulled from out of her and she started to straighten up to stand, but stumbled and would have fallen head first, had he not gripped her around the waist to steady her still shaking, trembling body.

Amusement clearly evident in his voice, he asked, "Are you alright, are you okay?"

Taking in a breath, she said, "I am okay, I am fine. Whoa!"

He laughed aloud as in sync; the two of them began to straighten up their clothes.

## The Stranger who took me from Behind

"My goodness," he said, his dark eyes staring at her partially-unbuttoned cream-colored cotton top. The diamond studs in his ears sparkled in the light from the television as he tossed his cap onto the nearby coffee table. He seemed not to know what to do with his hands, or maybe he was nervous as he rubbed both hands down the legs of his pants. Continuing on with his conversation, he said, "I cannot believe that you want a reduction. They are beautiful. If you don't mind me asking, what size are they?"

"Forty-two double D," she said with a small grin. Shifting on the couch, she happened to glance at the clock on the wall, and then said, "You know I really should be going."

"Why?" he asked. "Is there somewhere you really need to be going? Could I offer you anything to drink?"

Noticing that he spoke to her chest, she laughed aloud and said, "No, I am fine." Tilting her head to the side, her dark brown eyes looking at him, she thought to herself, "Hmm...it has been seven months since I had a hard cock between my thighs."

He was not overly bad looking, just not usually what she went for. Although two years younger then her, she knew that he was out of her league and had a world of experience. Instinctively upon meeting him, she had known this. He had nice eyes, though, and his skin was the color of rich milk chocolate. Chocolate had always been her downfall and, as predicted, she was slowing sinking. Suddenly, smiling really wide and feeling a bit wild, she said, "If I let you touch them, will you let me go?"

"Will you want to go afterwards?" he asked, scooting closer to her. His fingers quickly went to the buttons of her top and began to unfasten them. Finishing, he spread her shirt open as one of his hands dipped into the cup of her white bra. "I want to see them," he said. She pulled both of her bra straps down and let him look his fill.

"Oh my," he said, then leaned down and lifted one to his mouth to gently kiss, then suck, the pointed tip of one tit. Meanwhile, his other hand played with her other breast. She hissed in a breath and arched her back as he began to kiss and suck on both breasts almost simultaneously. A second or two later, he lifted his head and captured her mouth under his. His lips were warm against hers and she tasted the beer that he had consumed earlier on them, although it wasn't overly unpleasant. He rubbed his tongue against hers as his kisses deepened.

She had just licked his bottom lip when she felt his hands unsnap and unzip her corduroys. She moaned into his mouth when one of his hands slid into her panties and smoothed down through her black curls. All of a sudden he pulled away from her mouth and moved to pull both her panties and pants down at the same time. She tilted her hips forward to accommodate him and he pulled both garments down to her knees. His hand then returned to her curly black thatch.

It had been far too long since she had been touched and she craved it, yearned for it. When his hand slid through the curls and he stuck a finger inside of her, she actually groaned aloud. It felt that damn good! One finger went inside of her, and then two as his mouth played with hers.

Five minutes later, maybe less, she found herself bent over the couch, both hands on the cushions for balance. She struggled to breathe as his hands gripped her hips, as a thick condom-covered cock speared up inside of her. She trembled in his grip, thinking that she had never ever had a cock this big, this massive, between her caramel thighs before. She had no control over the depth of his thrusts as he dominated her, leaning over her to go even deeper. Her small opening struggled to accommodate his length, her muscles clamping tight as first, until her wetness began to ease his passage.

She couldn't believe that this was happening to her; she had just met him that night. They had talked for about an hour and now she was getting fucked out of her mind by him. She, who had always been rational in the past, had never done something this crazy before. She, who had always protested when an ex-lover had wanted to take her from behind, was letting a stranger do just that.

"Oh heck," she thought to herself, "I don't even know his last name." Then she stopped thinking when he hit just the right spot.

## The Black Warrior

He glanced over at her lounging on the couch watching the television avidly, a television tray sitting in front of him. Popping a French fry into his mouth, he chewed and then took a sip of the drink at his right elbow.

He swallowed then he asked, "Comfortable?"

"I am quite comfortable," she said her dark brown eyes full of merriment as she smiled at him.

"Hmm"...he said. Eyes sober, his expression quite serious, he continued speaking "I am going to fuck you good tonight. I am going to fuck you again and again, hard. I hope that you can handle it. I really hope that you can handle it, all of me! I am going to give you every inch of my cock, all twelve inches!"

Taking her gaze off the television, she shifted on the couch and turned towards him. Tilting her head to the side, she said, "I want you to fuck me good! I can handle it, I can handle you! Bring it on, mister!"

She sat up and began to undress, unbuttoning her thin sheer blouse. Reaching around and unsnapping her black bra, she tossed the items aside. Rising to her feet, she rolled black, knee length spiked boots down off of her smooth, shiny legs. French pedicure toes stepped out of them and then carried her over to where he sat on the opposite couch. Not saying a word, but holding her gaze the entire time, he moved the tray out from in front of him. She spread her legs slightly and used her knee to open up his closed legs. She moved to stand between his legs, when they opened up for her.

He pulled up her short blue skirt and then combed his fingers through her already moist black curls. He shoved 1 finger, then 2 up into her wet pussy. She sighed, swaying on her feet as his fingers moved inside of her wetness, slowly, then faster and deeper.

It became all too much for her a minute later and she fell to her knees to the floor, grabbed his sweatpants with both hands and ripped them down his caramel legs. He tilted his hips to accommodate her, sensing her hunger, her desperation. Holding his big cock in one hand, he placed the other one in her hair to guide her head towards his cock. Reaching his cock, she opened her soft pink lips and he removed his hand from around his cock. Licking the soft, plump head of his cock, she circled her tongue around it. Dipping her tongue into the little eye, she tasted the wetness that had gathered there.

Groaning, he reached down and cupping her chin in both of his hands, tilted her face up towards him. Looking into her questioning dark brown eyes he said "Open your mouth wider, take my big black cock deeper into your warm mouth."

She cupped his round butt in both hands and tilted his hips up towards her mouth. Opening her mouth wider, she went down further onto his girth and he swore, his hands inevitably tightening in her hair. He started to grow bigger and bigger in her mouth, and she struggled to take all of him. Her tongue drew circles down the length of it for a second longer, and then she reached up and pulled his hands from out of her hair. Wrapping her small hands around his great length, she leaned down to kiss and suck at his balls. He groaned, his thighs tightening; as she leaned down further to lick his ass hole.

Shaking slightly, she sat up on her knees and said, "Turn around."

He turned around and she licked her lips, his perfect caramel colored butt was smack dead in front of her mouth. Placing both hands onto his butt, she pushed at him, forcing him to lean over and grip the couch as she began to feast. Biting, licking at the round globes, she was in ecstasy, he smelled so damn good, she thought to herself, as she ran her tongue gently along the crease where both of his cheeks met.

He swore, saying, "Oh shit!" He had never seen her like this before. It both surprised and thrilled him all at the same time. He let her enjoy herself for a minute more, and then he pulled away from her wet mouth.

"Lie down," he told her, brown eyes holding hers and she complied.

"Spread your legs wide, he told her, really wide."

She spread her legs and he gripped her thighs in both hands and lowered his head. She had one brief moment to notice the glimmer of his diamond stud earrings in the faint candlelight just before his tongue licked the tiny nub between her thighs. She shook and attempted to close her legs but he wouldn't let her. His hard hands gripped her soft thighs and spread her even wider as his mouth went to work on her.

Trembling, hips moving, she wiggled in his grip, pleading with him to stop, then to don't stop. Embarrassed as her wetness started to drip out of her pussy into his open mouth, she pleaded with him again. He ignored her for a few minutes longer, until finally he pulled away. Rising to his knees, he moved between her spread legs and told her to grab a hold of her ankles.

"Keep yourself open to me, legs spread wide so that I can give you every inch; give you this big black cock. I am going to fuck you good."

He guided himself into her, after telling her this, holding his enormous girth in one hand. Her entire frame shook, back bowed; chest lifting up as her tiny, tight pussy was invaded by him. She struggled to adjust to his size, breathing hard, as his hips began to move. His light brown eyes stared into her dark brown ones as she trembled in his grip.

Holding her immobile in his grip, he whispered to her. "I am going to penetrate you again and again tonight! I want you to suck it, make it harder, and then I am going to cum inside of you again and again. You want this, don't you?"

Her tits shook with the force of his lunges, but she managed to breathe out, "Yes, I want this! I want your big cock inside of me!"

"I am going to give it to you too, he told her and I want for you to take it, take all of it!"

He moved inside of her a few minutes more, and then he pulled out of her dripping wetness. Cupping her head in both hands, he guided her towards his enormous cock.

Sitting down on the edge of the couch, he told her, "Suck it, suck it some more!"

She opened her mouth to comply and he groaned, as she licked him for a minute or two, then he pushed her back down and shoved his hard cock back inside of her. Three times that night, he did that, pulled out, had her suck him off, and then went back inside of her deep. His stamina was unbelievable; she struggled to keep up with him, pleading with him to cum.

He wrapped his hands around her wrists, to hold her down and face fierce, he informed her, "I will cum whenever I want to, you don't tell me when to cum. You feel too good to me, nice and wet."

But, when he leaned down to bite at her hard pointed nipples, he shook and she knew that he was about to cum then. She was right too, because he pulled away from her and began to cum. He thrust his hips forward and went even deeper inside of her to make sure that she received each and every drop of his creamy semen. When he finally stopped cumming and pulled away from her soft body, she lay there trembling, thighs shaking.

Lying there on the blanket, struggling to still her shaking body, she knew that she would never be the same. Her body would never be the same, he had forever branded her. The black warrior that night had made her his completely. He had ruined her for every other man.

# Lights, Camera, Action

Leaning against the wall, she watched him walk towards her, his stride slow and lazy, black eyelashes covering hooded light brown eyes.

"Come on," he said in his low, sexy voice.

She turned and followed him into the brightly lit studio. He walked across the cement floor, turning off lights, cameras as he went further into the room, with her walking right on his Timberland heels. He checked the big exit door and then turned to her, and said, "I want to take you from the back; I want to have you from behind."

Breath catching in her throat, pussy swollen and wet, she turned around and unzipped her black cords. She wore no underwear beneath them. Bending at the waist, she locked her legs and waited for him to thrust into her. She felt one brush of cool air across her bare caramel butt, before his hard hands gripped her hips.

He pushed into her a second later and she shuddered, whole body shaking as he begin to fuck her hard. Her high heeled black boots skidded across the floor as he thrust deep into her. She started to make little noises as soon as his hard cock invaded her wet, tight pussy.

Smoothing a hand across her tailbone, he whispered to her, "Shh...you have to be quiet. Hey, where are you going?" He asked when her heels skidded across the floor once more. "Give me that ass!" and gripped her hips yet even harder.

Blood rushing to her head and shaking all over, she said, "Wait, I am falling. I am going to fall. Please, let me get that chair over there."

He stopped in mid thrust and pulled completely out of her, his cock making a popping sound as he pulled out of her dripping wetness. "Ok," he said and pulled his pants back up around his waist.

She carefully walked the short distance over to the chair, pants still around her ankles. Reaching the chair, she leaned over it, bracing her hands on the arms of it. He dropped his pants, separated her caramel round twin moons with his hands and thrust his cock back up inside of her warm, welcoming wetness. Biting her bottom lip, eyes drifting closed, she swallowed a moan. She was in sheer ecstasy, this is what she wanted. This is what her body needed, what it craved. The rawness, the very idea of it being forbidden and the exciting thrill of getting caught.

He had only been thrusting for a few seconds more, when suddenly she heard a noise. Her body instantly went still, eyes flying open and she started to raise her upper body. Turning her head to the side, she whispered, "Did you hear that? I think that I just heard something?"

His hands had fallen to grip at her hips the instant that she had moved. "Hey, he whispered, where the hell do you think that you are going? Bring that ass back to me, give me that ass!"

Her whole body trembling, she said, "I heard a noise, didn't you hear it? Stop, please stop for a minute!"

Letting out a groan, he stopped his thrusts and went still. The noise came again and this time he heard it too as well. It was closer this time, she was sure of it.

"Oh, he said, that is just the camera crew. They should be walking in here in a few more minutes. I am not going to let you go though! You can forget about it! My cock is as a hard as a rock and your pussy is warm, wet. I am to fuck you until I fill you with all my cream! I don't care about them!"

Eyes growing wide, she started to sputter a protest, when he placed his hand onto the small of her back and pushed her back down once again. She started to fight him then, in an attempt to get away.

Body twisting, she struggled with him, but he wouldn't let her get away.

His hands moved back up to cup her shoulders and he used his thumbs to hold her head down. As he began to thrust back into her hard, he whispered, "You still have your blouse on. You knew the risk, when you came here! The risk of the possibility, that we might get caught. Your hair is covering your face, just keep your head down and they won't see your face. You are going to take me, all of me!"

The lights flashed on then, just as he spoke the last word and although she didn't dare look up, she heard the footsteps. Then, the two male voices exclaiming in almost unison, "Dang man! You are really giving it to her, aren't you? Don't stop on our account, keep going!" She heard him utter a short burst of laughter, then she heard the snap of the cameras. Hips moving rapidly, he thrust one last time into her hard, and then he went still. His hips jerked once, and then twice against her bottom, as he began to cum. His semen, warm from his body, shot into her deep.

He pulled out of her immediately afterwards, pulling his boxers, pants back up. He laughed as he snapped and zipped his pants up. Face hot, she reached down and pulled her pants back up shaking legs to the sounds of catcalls and whistles.

## *Pussy & Boots*

Sitting on a desk across from where he was seated, she gestured to him with her hands. She swung her boot clad legs as she talked to him. Her dark brown eyes sparkled as she spoke, her right hand reaching up occasionally to brush a lock of her dark brown shoulder length hair back behind her ear. When she uttered something which she thought was quite witty, she would toss her head back and laugh loudly.

Looking up from his paperwork occasionally to give her an answer or two, he thought to himself, "My word, she is beautiful."

His green eyes watched as she paused for a breath and licked her full red lips, then resumed her conversation. He barely bit back a groan when he saw the pink tongue slip out to moisten her upper, then lower lip. Suddenly shifting around to face him, she crossed her boot-clad legs, making her knee length brown multi-colored skirt rise up higher to exposing her pantyhose covered thighs. After making herself comfortable, she crossed her arms across her ample chest and continued on with her animated conversation.

"So then," she said, "You would never believe it, but...." Her voice trailed off as she suddenly realized that he had gone quiet all of a sudden, the paperwork lay forgotten in from of him. He sat, just staring at her, not saying a single word.

Her dark brown eyes blinked, and then she asked, "What? Why are you just sitting there staring at me? What is it?"

Shaking his head at her, he stood up and pushed back his chair and walked towards her. Moving to stand directly in front of her, his green eyes locked with hers as he said, "It is nothing, but you are so damn beautiful. Sexy and you don't even realize it. That's what makes it so unbelievable, so very special."

She laughed nervously, then said breathlessly, "My, but you are full of flattery all of a sudden. I am just little old me. There is nothing extraordinary about me; nothing special. Move away from me, you are making me nervous."

Uncrossing both her legs and arms then, she shifted on top of the desk again, leaning back from him and placing the palms of her hands flat on the desk. Ignoring the gathering moisture between her thighs, her tongue flickered out once again to lick her lips as she waited to see if he would do as she had asked for him to do.

"For Pete's sake, stop doing that," he said genuine frustration in his voice. "Oh, the hell with it!"

Both of his hands reached down all of a sudden and pushed her thighs apart. She gasped, her dark brown eyes opening wide as he stepped between her spread thighs, one hand going down to cup her right bottom cheek, bringing her body in closer contact with his. His other hand went up to tangle his fingers in her dark brown strands as his mouth crashed down onto hers. He kissed her then, his tongue licking the closed seam of her mouth, urging her to open her tightly sealed lips. He licked the seam a second time, then he pulled away.

Moaning, she opened her eyes to stare into his as he whispered, "Open up. Let me inside."

"No," she started to say.  As his tongue slid between her lips, it was then that she realized her mistake. Moaning, her eyes fell closed once again as she shoved her hands into his hair and gave in. Their lips clung together as they drank from each others mouths for a few, then she gasped when he suddenly pulled his mouth away from hers, swearing.

Her eyes flew open wide, as he said to her, "Fuck this, I got to have you now! I need to get inside you. I am about to burst."

Her shiny, wet mouth opened in shock as she felt him reach down between their bodies to lift her skirt up around her waist. Ignoring her gasp, he shoved both hands into the top of her pantyhose and pulled them down so that they rested on the top of her tall boots.

Falling back onto the desk, shaking, she gasped out, "What...what are you doing?"

He didn't answer; he was too far gone. His face was flushed, his breathing harsh. She watched as he pulled down his zipper, shoved his boxers down and pulled out his swollen cock. Then he started to move back between her legs. When he found that he could not because her pantyhose prevented him from doing so, he cursed.

"Fuck," he said. Then she watched in disbelief as he lowered his head and, using his teeth, he tore at them.

He paused long enough to say to her, "Damn, you smell good."

His nostrils were flaring at the scent of her arousal as he went back to his task of destroying her pantyhose. After making a tear in them, he used his hands to finish ripping them off of her trembling caramel colored thighs. As soon as he finished ripping the last piece of hosiery out of his way, he spread her thighs wide and shoved himself into her wetness.

She fell back onto the desk with a moan, her body arching as her boot-clad legs wrapped themselves around his hips. Cupping her bottom in both hands, he pulled her closer to him as his hard, swollen cock sank deeper inside of her small, drenched opening. She shoved both hands into his hair when he leaned down to kiss her. His hips began to move.

Through the thin fabric of her blouse, he felt her hard pointed nipples stab into his chest each time he thrust into her and he swore that it made his cock get harder.

'Inside of her... inside of her... have to get inside her,' he thought to himself as his tongue drove down her throat and his cock drove inside her wet, warm pussy.

A minute or two later, it all became too much for her. She pulled her mouth away from his and screamed aloud. He thrust once, then twice more into her; and then shot his load inside of her.

He laid atop her body for a minute or two to catch his breath, as she smoothed her hands across his shoulders and back. Then he pulled away from her. The minute he pulled away from her body, she promptly reached up and slapped him across the face and eyes.

"What the hell was that for?" He asked, grabbing her wrist, his green eyes spitting fire.

"Damn you," she said. "You destroyed a brand new pair of pantyhose in your hurry to get between my legs!"

Letting go of her wrist, he rolled her over onto her stomach and slapped her bare bottom with his hand once, then twice.

After the last slap, he said, "Might of funny, I didn't hear you complaining after I got between them caramel thighs, though. Shit, you were soaking wet. In fact, I would put money on it that you were creaming your panties as you were talking to me. You are a little tease! You wanted me just as much as I wanted you! You are just trying to deny it! Your body tells the real story, though!" After saying all of this, he pulled away from her and began to straighten his clothes.

Bottom smarting, she rolled back over and pulled her skirt back down to cover her thighs. She knew that he was right, even though it made her angry that her body would betray her.

# Two Cum Together

"What are you doing? You are keeping so much noise, I can barely hear you," she said, a blue cell phone pressed against her right ear. Snuggled under a pile of bedcovers, propped up against a couple of green satin pillows, she had been talking to him for about a good twenty minutes now.

His voice slightly muffled, called back to her over the speaker phone, "I am about to take a shower."

"A shower, is that what you said?" she asked, a smile evident in her voice.

"Yeah, that is what I said. It would be nice if you were here to join me," he called back to her.

"You are silly; I am thousands of miles away from you. But, hmm…" she said, "You just gave me a really great story idea."

"Really?" he said. "A story about what? Tell me about it."

"Well...I was thinking, well you know about two people getting wet. You in the shower and I in bed...No, never mind. Perhaps I should not speak of such things. It is impossible, after all, for us to be together right now."

"No," he said, "Tell me."

She could hear the genuine intrigue in his voice now.

"I really don't think that I should tell you...because," she paused.

"Come on, tell me. Don't stop now, you are teasing me," he said.

"Well, alright, I guess that it will be okay. I will tell you what I was thinking about...You getting wet, water sluicing, slippery wet over your mahogany skin...and between my caramel thighs, warm moisture gathering..." she paused once again.

"Go on, I want to hear all of your naughty thoughts. Please tell me more..." he pleaded with her, his voice barely audible above the roar of the shower.

"Okay," she said. "But first let me take my tee-shirt and panties off, though. I am going to have to put the phone down for a second, okay?"

"Yeah," he said. "You do that. Come right back though; don't hang up."

She could hear the interest in his voice as he waited in anticipation of what would be said or done next.

Kicking off the suddenly stifling bedcovers, she laid the phone on the bed and removed her items of clothing. A second or two later, she laid back down on the bed and propped herself back up against the pillows.

Letting out a little laugh, she said, "Now where was I?"

"You were about to tell me the rest of the story idea," he said. "Stop torturing me."

She laughed and said, "Okay, yeah now I remember. Imagine me joining you in the shower, naked as the day I was born. You are quite taller then me, so I will let you soap the top part of your chest, but I will do the rest. Slide my slippery hands down your chest, across the swell of your stomach and down each thigh. Spread your legs a bit, so that I can run my fingers along the crease of your buttocks, massage the cheeks of your ass." She paused then for a minute.

"Keep going," he said, his voice pleading. "Don't stop now. What are you going to do next?"

"Wait a second while I spread my legs wider," she said, shifting on the bed.

"Girl you are something else," he replied. "I am getting hard just thinking about that sweet pussy. Remember when I went down on you to kiss your pretty pink, vanilla scented lips. You do remember that my favorite kind of ice cream is vanilla, don't you? Are you stroking yourself down there or are you playing with those caramel tits with the big chocolate brown nipples? Remember how strongly I sucked those nipples in my mouth; I could have eaten you alive. Pure sweetness."

"Shut up and listen," she said. "This is my story; my fantasy. Stop taking over the story, I want us to cum together, not separate. You better stop saying all of that nasty stuff, before you make me cum. I am getting so wet."

He laughed aloud, then said, "Go on, girl. Damn you are good at what you do. Tell me more. I need to hear more."

"Feel my hands slide down each leg. Stand on one leg and put your hands on my shoulders, while I kneel in front of you to wash your feet. I will wash each foot, making sure to slide my fingers in between your toes to clean them. Then, I will stand to my feet afterwards and have you step under the spray of the water to rinse the soap off."

He interrupted her once again to say, "Wet your index finger in your mouth and circle your nipples for me. Cup one of your tits in one hand and bring it up to your mouth; lick and bite at the nipple. Imagine that it is my mouth wrapped around it suckling you. You still have those satin sheets? Rub the bottom or the top sheet across your hard nipples for me."

"Damn you," she said, her voice dropping a few octaves. "Let me finish. This is my story, not yours." With the phone still pressed against her ear, she shifted once more to turn over onto her stomach. Tossing the pillows to the floor, she laid the front of her body against the bed flat. Then, getting up on her knees, she spread her legs and then aligned her body so that her butt was raised high up in the air.

"Hey," she said breathlessly, "I am about to put you on speakerphone, okay? I am afraid that I need both hands free now."

He chuckled and said, "Okay, but you better not hang up the phone either!"

Angling her body so that her heavy tits lightly kissed the satin green sheet beneath her, she leaned on one elbow to brace the top of her body slightly upward. The aching wet place between her legs begged for satisfaction, so once more she returned a hand between her caramel thighs.

Stroking her gathering wetness with her fingers, she barely managed to speak. "Ah, ah, where was I? Oh yeah, now I remember, the water has washed all of the soap off of your body now and it is time for me to once again kneel in front of you. Pressing you back against the wall of the shower, I am to going to cup the cheeks of your ass in both hands. Your cock, hard and swollen, is winking at me, just begging to be licked, kissed and sucked. I am so hungry for it to be in my mouth. I want to taste it, drink from it, and run my tongue up and down its length. Your hands gather in my hair to hold me close as you let out a groan at my first wet lick. The warm steamy water falls forgotten over our slippery wet naked flesh. Take your cock in your hands, do it now! I want to hear you jerk off, to hear your shout of release in my ear. Cum for me, I want to hear each and every groan. Imagine my fingers running along the crease of your ass, as I cup you closer, so that your cock almost hits the back of my throat."

She thought that she heard him murmur something like a reply back to her, but she was no longer listening. Bottom lip pulled between her front teeth, two, then three fingers drove deep into her wetness. She imagined a long hard, cock going in and out and her breathing became ragged. Suddenly her muscles clamped down around her fingers as she began to cum. In her subconscious mind, she vaguely thought that she heard his groan of release, but she wasn't quite sure. Screaming aloud, she lost her balance and fell flat faced down on the bed, arms landing at her sides. Eyes closed she turned her head to the side struggling to gasp some air back into her deprived lungs. Finally getting some air back into her lungs, she took the phone off of speakerphone and put the phone once more back up to her ear to ask, "Did you cum?"

She heard nothing for a few seconds but the rush of the water, then the water being turned off.

"Are you still there?" she asked.

"Yeah," he said his breathing harsh. "I had to wash off again. Didn't you hear me cum? Hell, I probably woke up the guests next door up for all that I know of. I think that is the longest that I have cum in a long time. My cream just kept shooting out of me. Damn, you are something else. I had to take another shower after all that naughty talk. I don't think that the hotel management people will be too happy with me.

They will probably charge me extra for taking an hour and a half shower. I heard you cum too, you sweet little nasty thing."

She laughed mischievously and said, "My legs are still open, cum on inside if you dare. Goodnight, I am going to sleep now, still naked, sweaty and wet." She disconnected the call then, without even waiting for his reply.

## Pass the Paper Please

I walked into the copy machine room last night and he was there. I don't know what made me to do what I did next; maybe it was because he stared at me with his wicked green eyes for a second. I don't know, maybe the devil made me do it. The minute he turned back around, his back to me as he began to shuffle some papers, I made my move. I picked up the clipboard and deliberately dropped it onto the floor, so that it landed by his feet. He immediately turned back around in startled surprise, and started to bend down to pick up it.

I stopped him, though, saying, "Stop. Don't you dare pick that up; I dropped it, so I will pick it up."

I moved closer to him, his green eyes locked with my dark brown eyes but he did not move a muscle. Stopping directly in front of him, I slowly bent down in front of him. I started to pick the clipboard up but changed my mind at the last minute, instead placing

one hand flat on the floor for balance, I placed my other

hand in between his feet and started to slide it up

between his legs, slowly traveling it up the inside of

his right leg. He sucked in a startled breath

and attempted to shift to the side, but then I moved

closer to him. My hand began traveling up his leg and

continued to his thigh, until I was about an inch from

his crotch. I stopped my hand then, but kept it where it

was as I slowly started to rise to my feet. I paused for a

minute, my face directly in front of his crotch as I eyed

the zipper for a second, debating whether or not I

wanted to attempt to pull it down with my teeth. He

seemed to stop breathing for second, waiting to see

what I would do. I licked my lips slowly and then tilted

my head back to see smoldering green eyes staring

directly at me, his mouth slightly parted, nostrils flared.

I laughed then and pulled my hand away. I then rose to

my feet, letting my front brush against his. My

hard pointed nipples pressed against his chest, but I backed away from him.

"A damn tease," he called after me as I walked out of the copy room. The clipboard still lay on the floor forgotten.

Later that night, he walked me to my car as usual. Upon reaching the parking lot, I discovered that I had parked behind a mini van. I debated for a minute, and then decided to do what I had really wanted to do all night. I grabbed his hand and pulled him towards the front of my car, so that we were in between the two vehicles. Using my hips, I backed him up against the front of my car. I then shoved my hands into his hair and moved in to kiss him. Slowly, I first licked his bottom lip with my tongue, then his top one. I was enjoying myself, loving the taste of him I must confess, until he hissed in a breath and grabbed me around the neck. I let out a moan into his mouth as he mashed his lips with mine. Finally fed up with my

teasing licks I guess...

## *Explosive*

I amazed myself that night as he made love to me all through the night. I never knew that my body could be capable of such activity, such pleasure. I think that he came inside of my body about four times that night; I lost track after a while.

The first time he pushed his way inside it hurt a bit, but then the pain passed as my body opened to receive him. My toes were pointed towards the ceiling, my legs in a "v", his arms wrapped around my thighs so that my legs lay against his chest. He stuffed his cock deep into my aching and still somewhat small opening. He had told me that he might not be long, but he was thick and it was this thickness that I craved as I moved my legs down his body to enclose his pumping hips. What really blew my mind though is when he pulled out and, spreading my thighs wide with his hands, lowered his dark head and began to eat me out. Just when I thought that I was going to go crazy, my hips lifting up helplessly towards his mouth, he would stop and shove his cock back into my supersensitive opening. I almost lost my mind, my body jerked and bowed under his, my tits shook with the force of his lunges. Still inside of me, he leaned down to kiss me, ravaging my mouth with his. I moaned as I sucked his long tongue inside my mouth. Pulling back, he gave me a little grin, his hazel eyes staring into mine, as he said, "You are going to curse at me tomorrow when you are hurting."

I said, "I do not care. Do not stop; please do not, baby."

Sweat dripped down from his brow as he pulled away from my mouth and once again pulled my hips tighter to his pumping ones. My legs rested against his shoulders as he arched his neck and began to cum inside of me. After cumming inside of me, he cleaned me up, using a wipe to wash away his residue. He tossed the cloth aside, and then stretched out to lie on his stomach and spread my legs wide, so that his face could rest in between them. Using his hands, he opened the lips of my vagina and begun to lick me, his tongue circling my clit, the nub of flesh in between and the opening where his cock had went in. I went crazy and attempted to close my thighs, but his shoulders prevented me from doing so. My body jerked as I felt him put his whole face against me so that he could brush his slight beard to tease at my flesh. My body arched, my hands pulled at his hair as my hips lifted towards his face. I thought that I was going to go insane. He pulled away, then began to slowly, lightly lick the tops of my thighs and the place right above my tight pubic curls.

We rested in between sessions; the front of his body pressed against my back, my head rested on his right arm, our right hands clasped together. His left arm wrapped around my body as his left hand smoothed across the lower swell of my stomach. When I wanted him again, I turned over onto my back, leaned up to kiss him and allowed my legs to fall open so that his hand would fall between my thighs and begin to stroke my gathering wetness. Then the whole process started all over again.

## *An Innocent Seduction*

Smiling at her, he reached for the antibacterial wipe that she pulled out of the small packet. She smiled and shook her head, saying, and "Uh-uh. I want to do it."

"Okay," he said and gave her a small grin, his blue eyes twinkling. Leaning closer to him she slowly brushed the cloth over his face, then ears, and around his neck. Then, cupping both of his hands in hers, she moved the cloth over each one of his hands. He did not move a muscle but watched her with narrowed eyes, a sure sign that he was aroused and she smiled at this. She tossed the cloth aside a few seconds later and leaned into him. He reached for her with one hand and started to pull her head towards him, but she cupped both of her hands around his face and kissed her way up his jaw. His arms went around her; while both of his hands reached down to cup her ass. Upon reaching his right ear, she nipped it between her lips.

"Ouch," he said. "What the hell was that for?" He jerked away from her, holding his ear with one hand.

"For torturing and taunting me repeatedly and making me beg for your kisses, damn you," she said.

"Turnabout is fair play," he said and pulled her closer to him and nipped her right ear as well.

"Ouch," she said then pulled his face down to meet hers and they kissed hungrily a moan escaping from her throat as she sucked his bottom lip between her full lips. Pulling back for a breath a second later, trembling slightly, she opened her dark brown eyes to stare into his blue eyes. Licking her lips, she said, "Thanks, but you know what I want."

"What do you want?" he asked, cupping the back of her neck with one hand, a small grin on his face. He knew what she wanted but he always made her ask for it anyway just to goad her.

Her eyes fell to his lips and she said, "Kiss me again, please, but deeper."

He laughed aloud, but then pulled her head towards him. Her head fell back onto his right shoulder; as he cupped her face with one hand and leaned down to meet her eager, greedy, waiting mouth. Her dark brown eyes fell closed as soon as his lips touched hers. As she felt his warm tongue curl its way into her mouth, she moaned once again and opened her mouth wider to invite him inside for a better taste. He pulled his mouth from her wet one a few seconds later, just when she had started to get lightheaded. Cupping her face in his hands, he said, "You know what you are? A little tease. You are a bad girl."

"You like it though; all of the badness, that is."

"Hmm..." he said. "Maybe I do, but we better stop regardless, unless you want to be laid down on this seat.

"'Kay," she said and smiled at him, then curled up against his chest. Her head on his shoulder, she placed an arm around his waist.

"Okay, what?" he asked turning her face up to his with one hand.

"Okay, we will stop," she said and giggled, leaning up to place a quick kiss on his chin. He laughed, and then cupped her neck with one hand, while his other hand went under her loose shirt to rub her bare back, occasionally letting his hand drop from under the shirt to smooth across her ass. They sat silently for a minute or two, savoring the forbidden temptation of wanting and needing satisfaction, but neither willing to risk the danger of being discovered. Closing her eyes and burying her face into his shirt, she savored the sensations: his hardness against her softness, the cool night air blowing through the window. Involuntarily, a yawn escaped her. He must have felt it against his chest, because he cupped her face up to his and said,

"There ain't no way in hell I'm going to let you fall asleep on me."

She yawned once again, laughed, and then said, "I will try not too, but it is your job to keep me up though. You make me feel so safe and warm; I love it when you hold me."

"Oh you do, huh? What makes you think that you are so safe with me?" he asked, staring into her eyes.

"Because you promised that you would never hurt me and I believed you," she said, staring back at him.

"I won't either, but I may decide to nibble on you just a little," he said, grinning. "Don't worry about falling asleep though, I will keep you awake," he promised. Then, cupping her face in his hands, he proceeded to kiss her senseless and, no longer sleepy, she responded with gusto.

## *Two Naughty Co-workers*

That night in the student center, I must confess, I was the one who started it. I wanted a kiss; so sue me. I had not been kissed in about three months and he looked quite kissable.

Therefore, that night when we walked into the office, I told him to come to me and I made him lean down so that I could kiss him. I only wanted a single kiss, but he was greedy and came back for more.

Pretty soon I found myself between the copier and the refrigerator, pressed against the wall being kissed senseless. I enjoyed it beyond belief.

His tongue swirled inside my mouth and stole the gum out of my mouth in mere seconds. My arms went around his shoulders, as he swirled his tongue inside my ear, then he licked his way down my neck. My breath hissed in as I felt him kiss the top of my breast, but what shocked the hell out of me is when he slid his hand inside my pants, inside my panties and touched the bare flesh between my legs. I jerked; my eyes flew open to stare into his hazel eyes.

He whispered, "Cum for me."

Shocked, fighting for breath, I said, "No. I can't."

"Yes you can," he said.

Then someone knocked on the door. He swore, then released me and went to answer whoever it was as I fell to my knees giggling with nervous relief, struggling to get my wits back.

Later that night he locked the door to the building, then followed me into one of the offices. Once inside the office, I realized that I hadn't replaced the paper towels in the adjoining restroom, so I went inside the restroom to replace them. He followed me inside and shut the door behind us. He switched the light on and backed me up against the sink. My butt hung half on and half off the sink as he began to kiss me senselessly. I moaned and arched up against him as my hands grabbed a hold of his head. He reached for the buttons on my shirt and, opening my top, pulled one of my bra straps down. Lifting one of my heavy breasts into his hand, he groaned and said, "I have been waiting to see this all night." He lifted it towards his mouth and began to suck the nipple. I arched my back, moaning, pressing his head against me as he fed.

A few seconds later his mouth returned to my mine, his tongue driving deep inside. He pulled from my mouth a few minutes later and his hand once again went inside my panties and burrowed through the tight curls at the top of my trembling thighs.

He watched me, his hazel eyes staring into my brown ones as I wiggled and went crazy in his arms. He relentlessly stroked my wetness for a few minutes. When his phone rang, he pulled away, swearing. He opened the door and walked out, but not before licking the "v" between my breasts, then trailing one finger in between them to spread the wetness. I felt like that he had left his mark on me when he did that, invisible as it may have been. I stayed in the bathroom breathing deeply, trying in an attempt to get myself under control after he walked out.

As soon as I walked out of the bathroom, he pulled a pen and a piece of paper from out of his pocket and said, "I swear you better call me."

## Ready and Willing

Last night I told him to bind me to his bed

I told him that I would willingly be his slave

I told him that I would do all that he asked

My body would become his for the completion of any

task

I told him to bind me to his bed

I informed him that I would willingly be his slave

I said, "Blindfold my eyes if you must,

For my body belongs to you," as I spread my legs in

complete and utter trust.

"Learn the shape of my lips; sample the taste of my

kiss

Sketch the curves of my body, my ample hips

Trace my full breast, my nipples, pebble hard, are

begging not to be missed."

Last night, I told him to bind me to his bed

I told him that I would willingly be his slave

Oh, my word, I daresay, we had loads of fun, as we

greeted the raising sun

Did I scream and beg for more? So many times, my

friend I lost track of score

# The Kiss

"He's asleep. I am telling you that he is out cold," Leslie said in a loud whisper.

"I want to wait a few more minutes," Irene whispered back leaning over and watching the slow rise of the masculine chest two feet from her nose.

"You are just trying to back out of it. I double-triple dare you to do it. The rum and coke did it; he is out for the count. I am telling you the truth, chicken," Leslie whispered loudly, staring at the handsome black, curly haired man in front of her.

"I am not a chicken; I am going to do it. I cannot do it though with you staring at me. Can I not get some privacy or something?"

Leslie laughed softly, rolled her eyes and said, "I am going, but you better do it. I want details tomorrow and do not even think about lying. Remember your annoying habit of twitching when you start to fib."

Irene straightened up; then, watching the face in front of her the entire time for any sign of movement, she moved forward. Slowly and very carefully, she started to straddle the legs of the man in front of her. Her black satin skirt slid up her thighs, exposing the top of her lace thigh high stockings as she finally sat down on the motionless man's lap. Licking her lips nervously, she slowly laid both hands on the hard chest in front of her for balance. Closing her eyes for a minute, she sat savoring the sensations. The hard tuxedo-clad legs pressed up to meet the soft, smooth bare flesh of her thighs. His heartbeat was steady and strong under her left palm.

Drawing in a breath, a smile touched her mouth as she inhaled the delicious scent of cologne... or was it aftershave? Oh, who the hell cared, he smelled wonderful. Letting out her breath, she opened her eyes and zeroed in on her target.

His face was relaxed in sleep, his full lips slightly parted; his long eyelashes covered the deep chocolate brown eyes hidden beneath. His chin was darkened slightly with just a hint of a beard. Moving in closely, she placed a kiss on the left cheek, where a dimple would be, had he been awake and smiling. A kiss was placed on the clef of his chin and one on his right cheek as well. Warming up to her activity, she leaned over and placed one gentle kiss on one set of long eyelashes, then one on the other. Placing a small kiss on his long nose, she finally reached his full mouth. Biting her lower lip nervously, she closed her eyes and took one slow lick of his bottom lip.

Drawing back, she opened her eyes suddenly. Had his breathing changed or had it just been her imagination?

Irene sat still for a minute, waiting and eyes wide. Then, determining that nothing had changed and that he was still sound asleep, she closed her eyes once more and leaned over. As she took a lick of his top lip, she could not stop the moan that escaped from her throat. The taste left upon her tongue was a mixture of rum, coke and pure man. She had to have more, to taste more and with that thought in mind, she leaned over, prepared to sample his entire mouth.

She had just placed her mouth gently on his, when all of a sudden two large hands buried themselves into her glossy dark brown strands. The once slack mouth began to move. She gasped and her eyes flew open. Oh, no! He was awake! His lips continued to move on hers, his tongue sweeping inside of her newly trembling mouth to taste her, while his deep chocolate brown eyes bore into her wide, shocked black ones.

## Rub Me the Right Way

"Where does it hurt?" he asked.

She turned her back to him and pointed to the right side of her neck and back. He placed both of his hands on the back of her neck and shoulders, beginning to rub her neck and tired, achy shoulder blades. Her body relaxed as his ministrations begin to take their affect. Her head dropped slightly forward as she exposed her neck to his hands, fingers. His right hand slipped down into her low top and brushed against her right breast. She leaned back into his embrace, allowing him to take her weight. Placing a hand onto his right thigh, she arched her back, as his fingers slipped into her white bra and touched her bare caramel colored flesh.

She let out a moan and tilted her head back and staring into his blue eyes, whispered, "Kiss me, please."

He kissed her, his tongue sliding between her parted soft lips and her dark brown eyes fell closed. She muttered a protest when he pulled away from her mouth a few seconds later, though.

"Ease up and slide this towel under your bottom. Tonight we are going to take it a bit further," he told her. His hands then went to the snap and zipper of her jeans. He unsnapped them and helped her pull them down a bit. One of his hands slipped into the front of her lacy white panties, his fingers burrowing through the top of her curly black thatch. Sliding his fingers through the slightly moist lips of her vagina wall, he began to stroke the awaking moisture.

Leaning back against him, she begged, "Go deeper. Please, you have to go deeper." One of her hands pressed down onto the top of his hand urging him to drive his fingers deeper inside of her hungry pussy. Her legs straightened out as she pulled her bottom lip between her teeth, her body trembling slightly.

"Fuck," he said, his blue eyes staring into her dark brown eyes. "You are tight."

Almost going over the edge, she became frightened and whispered, "Stop, please stop."

He drove two of his fingers deeper inside her for a second longer; then he relented and slowly drew his fingers out from between her trembling thighs. Breathing deeply, shaking slightly, she managed to pull her panties and jeans back up, moving the towel from beneath her bottom. He unzipped his pants then and pulled out his swollen, slightly red cock and placed her hand on it. Placing her small left hand around his thick cock, her thumb and index finger wrapped around the head. His cock was hot to her touch, as she at first stroked the head, watching it swell. She wrapped her full hand around it a second later and began to pump with her hand.

"Harder," he said. "Pump it."

Looking at his cock in genuine fascination, she asked, "Am I doing it right? I am not that experienced at this."

"Yes." His eyes closed as he breathed in and out. "Keep going, I am almost there. Don't worry about your experience; you are doing just fine, sweetheart."

This was a new experience to her; she had never watched a man cum before. A man had cum inside of her body before, but she had never watched it happen before now: watching a cock swell, increase in size, liquid glistening on its head. Her left hand tired, so she switched hands and used her right hand to continue to pump him. The tip of his cock was shiny now yet he still had not erupted. Pulling her bottom lip between her teeth, her brow wrinkled as she concentrated and wrapped both hands around his cock.

A few seconds later, she leaned over and placed his cock between the crease of her generously large breasts and he erupted.

"Fuck!" he exploded, his blue eyes flying open as his warm creamy white cum gushed out between her caramel globes. One hand still holding his cock, she jerked back in surprise because he had not given her any warning that he was going to cum. His cum dripped down into her white satin bra, as the rest of his warm cum filled her hand.

"You could have warned me!" she said, staring into his blue eyes, still in shock. He apologized to her and handed her a wet cloth to wipe his cum off of her. She dipped the cloth in between her breasts and began to wipe his cum away. He cleaned himself up quickly, and then began to wipe his cum from between her breasts himself.

Smiling slightly at her, he said, "I thought that was what you wanted."

"It is okay," she said. "Really." Showing that she forgave him, she reached up and wrapped her arms around him and kissed his cheek. His arms went around her and one of his hands gently tapped her butt.

## Quench My Thirst

"Are you sure about this? I mean, explain to me once again why you feel the need to resort these extreme measures? Damn, girl, were you or were you not listening to me when I told you about what Stephen did to me? That dumb ass just joined the rest of the 'ex's'. I am so sick of the male race in general now. But, hey, that's what I get for once again following my damn raging hormones instead of using some common sense for once in my life. Girl, don't make the same mistakes I have in my lifetime of dating losers. Physical attraction, lust, wherever the hell they call it now! Shit, why don't they just come right out and say, 'the urge to jump somebody's bones and have your wicked way with their body'? I am telling you though, seriously, make sure that he has half of a brain, too; because once the sex is gone, what the hell do you have left?"

She paused for a breath and took a long swallow of her Long Island ice tea. She sighed loudly, threw up her hands and said, "Alright, damn it, I will do it. I don't like it, but I'll do it. But remember this: you owe me big time and I will remind you of this sacrifice."

She pushed back from the table and stood up. Tossing her long, dark-brown (almost black) hair back over one shoulder, she said, "Watch my drink; or better yet, finish it off."

With these last words, she turned to walk across the room. Several male heads turned to watch her saunter towards the bar. On one barstool a lone, dark-brown haired man sat nursing a longneck; eyes focused on the big screen television high on the wall that blared out a hockey game. She walked right up to him, much to the disappointment of the other men. Stopping in front of him, she said, "Hi, handsome. Let me buy you another longneck. That one looks a little flat."

He glanced at her and said, "I don't think so, I just brought this one a few minutes ago. It tastes just fine to me." Giving her a sexy half grin, he turned his glance back to the television screen. She gave his handsome profile a smirk. She leaned over towards him, making sure that the left side of her breast brushed against his black tee-shirt that covered a muscular arm, and slipped the bottle out of his hands. The subtle brush of her breast against his arm had gotten his attention off the television screen.

He turned his head and watched her with narrowed dark-brown eyes. A half smile touched his mouth as he said, "Alright, sweetheart, you have my attention. Now that you have it, what are you going to do about it?"

Giving him a wink and a smile, she proceeded to take a long swallow of his beer. He said nothing, but watched her with his arms crossed across his chest. She took the bottle away, licked her lips slowly, taking her time.

"Yep," she said. "Just as I thought. Flat."

He followed the movement of her tongue with his eyes for a millimeter of a second, and then said, "Alright, baby, I'm game. You can buy me that beer that you promised.

At the end of the half hour, hungry black eyes having followed his every movement, he had shared a couple of more beers with the brunette. They moved their little party to the pool table in the corner. The plain woman seated at the table in the corner watched in envy as the dark haired man played pool with the brunette. After a few minutes, the brunette woman whispered something into the dark-haired man's ear and the two of them started towards the door. When the two of them passed the plain woman's table, behind the dark haired man's back, the brunette gave her a thumb's up sign.

Fast forward to an hour later....

Whispers could be heard: "Are you ready? If this wasn't so dangerous, I would laugh my ass off, but you are so serious, so I will try to be as well. Who knows, maybe we can laugh about this when we get old and gray, twenty years down the road. Believe me when I say that it was no easy task to get away from him in the first place; he wanted me, but he had drunk a little bit too much and was unable to stop me from leaving."

"Maybe we will laugh about this later. Thanks, Carrie. You are sure that he is out of it, right?"

Once the two of them got inside the dark masculine bedroom, they took a moment to let their eyes adjust to the dark, and then tiptoed over to the king-sized bed. Lying on the bed was a lone figure. He laid spread eagle with a single sheet covering his waist; the rest of his body was bare. The moonlight shining through the blinds reflected off his handsome features, relaxed in slumber: the long, dark-brown eyelashes that covered the dark eyes, the long straight nose and full mouth slightly parted.

Smiling at each other with delight, the two women quickly went to work. Pulling out their equipment from the black knapsacks on their backs, they quickly slapped one long strip of gray duct tape across his mouth. He jerked awake in alarm and started to sit up, but they subdued him, just barely. It took almost all of their strength to hold him down as they tied his arms and legs to the bedposts. When they finished, almost breathless, they sat down on the bed on each side of him to survey their handiwork. Angry dark eyes stared back at them, his nostrils flared. The sheet had slipped in their struggle of wills and the beautiful hard body was now on full display.

Carrie turned her head, looked at her and whispered, "Good luck, girl. He is all yours; enjoy. I will lock up." With those last words, she rose off the bed and walked to the door.

The other woman sat staring into those angry eyes for a minute then she whispered the following to him with a small smile, "I swear to you, I mean you no physical harm, yet I have come to fulfill a need. You don't understand, but soon all will be explained. I only pray that this one time will be enough to quench the driving hunger that makes me weak."

She shifted on the bed, pulled all of the covers off and began her journey of critical discovery. Slowly, she ran both hands through his dark hair, brushing the soft strands with her fingers, covering his beautifully shaped head. Shaping the outer curves of his ears with her fingertips, she leaned over and kissed the cleft of his chin which was roughed by a faint beard. Sliding down one side of his body, she placed her nose against the curve of his strong neck, inhaling the mixture of a light sweat and aftershave. She smoothed her hands across his hard shoulders, then drew back and reached for the bottle of peppermint oil beside her knee. Flipping open the top, she spread some on her hands, rubbed them together, and once more reached out like a bee driven to honey, seeking to touch his warm skin. Taking each of his hands in hers, she rubbed the oil on them, marveling at how big his hands were compared to her own. Once the oil had absorbed, she placed a kiss to the palm of each one and continued downward. Pouring more oil in her hands, she smoothed her hands down each one of his arms.

Then, straddling his hips, she leaned forward on her knees to rub oil on his lightly haired chest, her fingertips grazing his hard male nipples, her palms lingering on his hard stomach muscles. Dipping her head, she placed one small kiss to his belly button and rubbed yet more oil on her hands to smooth over his hard hips.

Out of the corner of her eye, she noticed that his once-sleeping cock had started to rise to attention. Licking her lips with a sudden burst of hunger, she lightly ran her tongue around the head. She felt him tense when he felt her wet tongue slide along him. He even appeared to stop breathing for a minute in the wake of it. His hard hips helplessly lifted towards her and his cock lengthened, begging for more loving attention.

She saw all of this and before she could stop it, a small burst of laughter escaped. She refused his pleading and continued on with her discovery. She took her time, exploring each muscular leg and his big feet. When she lifted her head back up to look at his body, she sucked in her breath at the perfection that lay spread before her. Unable to take her gaze away, she was almost hypnotized by the length of flesh jutting away from his body, the tip wet with one single drop of essence. Panting slightly, she managed to tear her gaze away and look up into the once-angry dark eyes, that were now filled with passion. She whispered, "Please, oh please, may I?"

But even though his eyes were almost glazed with desire, his hips trembling in their effort to stay still, he shook his dark head in quick denial.

Sighing, she drank from the bottle of water beside her right knee, replaced the cap and whispered, "But I fear that I must. The water doesn't even come close to quenching my raging thirst."

And with these words, she slid between his legs until her face was at just the right angle. She reached out her hands and searched through his dark pubic hair to cup his heavy sac in her hands, and gently rubbed it for a minute. And when she felt his hips jerk, she leaned down to taste what she had found, breathing deeply of his musty scent. Kissing her way around his heavy sac, she alternately grazed her fingertips in small circles on his balls. Involuntarily, his hips jerked up once again at the feel of her mouth working on him. His hard cock grazed her cheek, once again begging for attention, the tip starting to drip with wetness.

She smiled against his skin, when she heard the smothered moan coming from behind the duct tape. She ignored the length of flesh for a few more seconds, and then decided to take pity on him. She placed one final kiss on his heavy sac and reached underneath him to grab his hard buttocks with both hands. She stared for a second at the jutting length just waiting for her mouth and almost salivated at its perfection. It was big, engorged with blood, the tip slowly dripping with a white essence.

She shivered with delight and let out a low moan. Then, she quickly swooped down and captured the tip of his cock in her mouth and began to suck eagerly. Up and down, in and out she moved, all the while his cock seemed to expand with each brush of her mouth, causing her to open wider. She felt his buttocks clench tight and his hips began to move in time with her mouth. Occasionally, she would let the tip slide out of her wet mouth to alternately lick his length all the way down into his sweaty, tightly-curled pubic hair.

His whole body was tense. The sounds coming from his throat were incoherent, somewhere between a moan; a groan, maybe. She felt her own nipples, hard, hurting, chafing her bra and she knew that it was time to finish.

Quickly, she moved her wet mouth back to the tip of his cock. And it was not a moment too soon either, because a few seconds later, his whole body tensed. He strained at the bonds that restrained him, his back bowed, hips raised as he started to climax. Hot, wet, salty essence gushed into her awaiting hungry mouth. She stayed with him the entire time, struggling to swallow every single drop. But, as fate would have it, some dripped down her chin to be lost in the open scoop of her blouse, and to land in the valley between her full breasts. Yet, he still came some more, which she struggled to swallow, the tip of his cock at the back of her throat. Until finally, at last, he stopped, spent.

His body, slick with sweat and the heavenly essence of peppermint oil, relaxed back on the bed and she raised her head. When she scooted back up to straddle his hips, through the thin layer of her biker shorts, she realized with wonder that her panties were soaking. The relaxed weight of his penis between her legs felt wonderful, still slightly pulsating, she thought to herself. It would appear that they both had climaxed at the same time. She watched his face as he lay still for a minute until he slowly opened his eyes and looked up at her.

Still watching him, she slowly reached over and gently pulled the tape off his mouth. His voice echoed huskily as he said one word, "Wow!"

She blushed, smiled, and asked if he wanted some water. He nodded his head yes, and she lifted his head so that he could swallow the still-cold liquid. When he was through, she replaced the cap and started to speak, but he stopped her by reaching up to swipe at her chin with one hand. She shivered at his touch and struggled to breathe. He saw her reaction and smiled in amusement. Then he narrowed his eyes and dropped his hand saying, "You had some of me on your chin," showing her the small drop of liquid on his index finger. "Do you want it?" He asked with a smirk on his handsome face.

She was beyond caring how wanton, desperate or hungry she seemed and answered "Please, oh yes!" She had even started to lean forward in anticipation for the last little drop of his salty, yet sweet cum.

He pulled his hand back at the last minute and smiled. Still watching her, he wiped his hand on the sheet underneath him instead. "I don't think so. Untie me now and get the hell out of my house. You do have a wonderful mouth, so I won't call the cops this time. But, if I ever see you again, I am going to call the cops on your ass so fast. I am not a whore to be used and then tossed aside. Hell, for all I know you could be some kind of psycho or something."

"But...please let me explain," she started to say.

He cut her off and said, "You have twenty minutes to untie me and get the hell out of my sight, bitch, or I will scream my ass off. Oh, and one more thing: tell your friend Carrie that the same goes for her, as well."

Swallowing her tears, she hurriedly complied with his wishes and quickly untied him. She got her things together, praying that she did not leave anything behind and ran for the door. As she ran out of the house into the night, she thought to herself, 'Well as least I had that one night. It will have to suffice through the lonely nights ahead.'

## Private Time

Doffing her clothes, she adjusted the temperature and stepped in under the hot spray of the water. The steamy water sluiced down her tired shoulders. As she smoothed the soap over her curves, she thought of him. A few seconds later, she reached on the shelf for the bottle of shampoo. Squirting a small amount into her hands, she then raised her hands and proceeded to wash the shoulder length dark brown hair. As she worked the shampoo into lather, she thought of him. Arching her spine a minute or two later, to allow the water to run through her hair, her thoughts were on him.

Turning off the shower a few minutes later, she stepped out and reached for two towels. She dried off with one and wiped the steam from the mirror. Quickly towel drying her hair, she tossed the second one to the floor. As she began to smooth the creamy lotion over her skin, she stared into the mirror.

Damn, she thought to herself, this is getting serious. I am starting to think about him twenty-four hours a day. My sleep is never restful, for he haunts my dreams. The hands smoothing the lotion over my neck, arms, breast are his, not my own.

Shivering slightly, she let out a gasp as the glass clearly showed the evidence of her need; her breasts slightly swollen, nipples drawn into hard little points of desire. Closing her eyes tightly at the blunt evidence, the hands moved across the swell of her stomach to each leg. When the hands reached back up to meet at the "v" between her legs, the springy, yet soft pubic curls slightly glinted with moisture. Sucking in a breath, she opened her eyes and stared intently at the hands in the mirror. With her whole body tense in anticipation, legs slightly spread; she watched the hands in the glass.

Biting her bottom lip in uncertainty, she wondered what the devil's hands would do next. 'Sinner! Filthy slut, you,' she could almost hear her mother's voice whisper in her ear.

I cannot do this. I will not do this, she thought to herself. But, the body in the mirror would not be denied. It wanted... no, needed satisfaction now, or it would die. The devil's hands inched closer to the tightly curled curls and she shut her eyes closed once again. Her hands, once again, became his wicked hands, fingers exploring deep into un-chartered territory. Unavoidably, a long moan rose out of her throat, and her breathing turned harsher. He surrounded her, he had seeped into her skin, and he was in her. A few minutes later, she fell to the floor on her knees landing on the wet towel.

Thirty minutes later, dressed entirely in black, she saw him. Friendly and polite as always, he greeted her with his usual, "Hello, Ms. How are you doing tonight?"

The mask once again in place, she showed no emotion, her response was just as formal. But, the dark brown eyes caressed the tall, strong body in front of her. Dressed entirely in dark blue, with laced military style boots on the feet. The dark brown eyes saw the thick head of hair covering the beautifully shaped head. Eyes the color of the sky and the slightly thin, yet full kissable lips. He was, she had decided upon first meeting him, simply too gorgeous to be real. How could he not know the effect he had on her, or for that matter every other woman at their workplace? Did he realize that she ached to have her fill? When it came to him, she was willing to be his slave, to be used at will.

### Use Me

The sweet, sweet texture of your skin; the very essence of it is what I want to sink in

Your eyes brim with the emotions of an ignited desire and they beckon to me

Full lips tempt me, inviting me to drink of a potion made of complete and utter sin

One hand cups my face as one strong arm draws me in

Passion, it appears, has been unleashed

Forbidden, it may be, yet it has reached out and consumed me

Free to do what my heart desires, I submit willingly to you

Embrace, trace and taste, caress all of me, all that I am

My body is no longer my own, it belongs to your mouth, tongue, hands and soul

I am yours to command

## *Needy*

As soon as I walked through the door, he grabbed my hand and led me to the bed. Sitting down beside me on the bed, he cupped my face in his hands and began to kiss me, his tongue driving deep into my mouth. I could not breathe, yet I loved it, I must confess. Soon I felt myself lying on the bed. He pulled back from my mouth and made short work of the buttons on my shirt. His huge hands went directly to my breasts, rubbing at them through my satin bra. However, that was not enough for him. His hazel eyes stared into my dark brown ones and he said, "I have to see them; I want to lick, taste and suck them."

I smiled, sat up and unsnapped my bra, then lay back down. Clasping each of my tits in his hands, he licked the nipples of both. Cupping one tit up to his mouth, he let out a groan, then latched onto my nipple and began to suck. Struggling to breathe, I arched my back, spread my legs wide and wrapped them around his body. He sucked both of my nipples until they were bright red and sore. It hurt like something awful, but I did not stop him; I knew that he was hungry. He drew back from me, unfastened my skirt, and pulled it down, taking my panties with it. Then standing up, he tossed the items to the floor, quickly stripped all of his clothes off and laid his body gently down on top of mine. Catching his weight on his elbows, he said, "Let me know if I hurt you at any time."

"You are not hurting me," I said with a smile.

He kissed me, savoring my mouth before he began to lick his way down my body. He paid a lick to each nipple, and then kissed my stomach. I trembled, knowing where he was headed, wanting it too, but fearful that I may be able not to handle it. Then it was too late as his hands brushed through the tight black curls and I let out a moan. Using his shoulders, he pushed my legs wider and then moved so that his face was resting between the "v" of my legs. When I felt the first lick of his tongue, I let out a very unladylike groan; I could not help myself, and it felt so damn good.

I opened my legs wider and tilted my hips towards his lips and long wet tongue. As he started to eat me out, I grabbed a hold of the headboard and, throwing back my head, screamed out in ecstasy. Although embarrassed tremendously, I could not control myself, as my moisture drifted out of me into his open mouth. Eyes watering, gasping, I yanked at the pillow beneath my head and bit at it, in an attempt to muffle my screams and moans. I came hard, so many times that I lost count.

A few seconds later, he moved back up my body and rubbed my essence from his face onto my taut, pointed nipples. Then, he reached down and positioned himself at the entrance of my still-supersensitive swollen clitoris. I wrapped my legs around his hips as he slowly began to push his way inside. Our eyes locked, hazel staring into dark brown as finally he sunk all the way inside of me.  I gasped as I felt him almost

touch the tip of my womb.  His hands reached around

me and grabbed my ass, pulling me up to meet each

plunge of his hips.  Arching my back, my hands reached

up to grab a hold of the headboard again. It felt so

good and involuntarily my legs grasped him tighter.  His

hips slammed into mine and, leaning down to meet my

mouth with his, he reached up and placed his hands

over mine, wrapped on the headboard.  I came again, a

few seconds later, my moan captured by his mouth.  I

felt him cum a second or two later, his warm essence

shot into my inner cavity, as his body slightly shook

with the force of his climax.

## Cum for Me

I had no idea how much he really wanted me until the night I went to him. I was in complete awe at how fast he undressed me and began to lick his way down my body heading for my nether regions. I could not believe that this was happening to me, as I struggled to catch my breath. Upon reaching my black curls, he began to eat me out. Licking at me first, he then placed soft bites on the lips of my vagina walls. My legs straightened out, as my hands pushed at his shoulders, but he was relentless, he gave me no relief.

"Cum for me," he repeated over and over again, but I fought him. He tied my hands together with a piece of rope; not tightly, but still I pushed him away.

"Please," he said at one point, his hazel eyes staring into mine, but I refused him still. When he grabbed a hold of my head at one point with both hands, I felt general frustration, maybe even angry as both of his lips covered mine and drew my lips inside of his mouth as if to either take the breath out of me or to devour me.

He threatened to discipline me for not complying with his commands for me to come. I was turned on, I must admit, but I still refused to give into him. His hands stayed between my legs, caressing me all night, kissing me constantly on the lips and I loved it.

He tried to get me to spend the night, holding me close and laying his head on my chest, but I refused to give into his demands. Finally he gave up and decided to dress me back, but not before telling me to climb up onto to his face so that he could drink from my wetness one more time. I did and later he dressed me.

I had my legs in the air, in the shape of a "v" so that he could slide my panties back on and in place. Upon reaching the top of my thighs, he held the soft fabric away for a second and leaned his head down to nibble at the curls at the top of my vagina lips, letting me feel his teeth. I pushed him away, telling him that I had to go.

He said, "Okay, but only on one condition: I get to keep your panties."

I went home that night, for the first time in my adult life, with no panties on. I admit that he excited and turned me on beyond my imagination. I absolutely loved it when his big hands rubbed my back as his hazel eyes stared deep into mine.

## Fill Me Up

Lip to lip

Thigh to thigh

Make me open wide

Do me until the worlds' deepest rivers and oceans run

dry

Chest to breast

Tongue to tongue

Make me moan, make me sigh

Do me standing or as I lie

Eye to eye

Palm to palm

Make me cum

Do me until juice runs from my plum

Front to back

Back to front

Make me well done

Do me in the kitchen, on the living room floor, or

against the bedroom door

Sex to sex

Love to love

Make me groan, make me cry

Do me with or without a glove

## *Craving Satisfaction*

That hot summer night, she had dressed for seduction. It had been over two months since she had been fucked. The wee rabbit toy she had was cute, but it no longer satisfied her anymore. She wanted to be penetrated, no needed to feel stretched, invaded again.

Standing in front of the bathroom mirror, dressed in a blush colored lacy bra and panty set, she brushed her dark brown hair out straight. Then she pulled on a thin white top and a knee length green colored skirt. Just before slipping her pink toes into a pair of high heeled black sandals, she applied a light application of Revlon caramel foundation and some Dr. Pepper flavored lip gloss.

Hopping into her car, she turned Prince's "Purple Rain" on full blast and, gunning the engine, drove straight for his house. He let her in, greeting her with a shy hello. Smiling at him, she stepped inside and headed for her usual seat on the couch.

"Want a drink?" He asked, walking towards the kitchen.

"Sure," she said, settling down on the couch and crossing her bare legs.

Pouring two tall glasses of coca-cola for her and him, he walked back towards her and handed her a glass as he sat down beside her.

Taking a sip of the cold drink, she placed it down onto the coffee table in front of her. Looking at him out of the corner of her dark-brown eyes, she smiled and asked, "So are you going to talk to me this time or, once again, will you play the shy one with me?"

"I will try and talk to you this time," he said, giving her a sheepish grin.

They talked for a few minutes; she carried on most of the conversation as usual. Then he fell silent and turned his attention back to the television.

Exhaling a breath, she said, "Damn it!" Then before he could even blink, she scooped her skirt up with one hand and settled herself onto his lap.

He started to ask, "What the hell?"

Cupping his face with both hands, she said "Shut the hell up!" and covered his mouth with hers.

"Kiss me back," she demanded, nipping his left ear with her teeth. Recovering from his initial shock, he shoved one hand into her dark brown strands and the other hand swept under her skirt. His mouth opened under hers, his tongue sweeping inside of her soft parted lips. One hand held her head captive for his tongue, while the other hand slid to the front seat of her panties and cupped her through the thin lace. Moaning into his mouth, she spread her legs wider, giving him easier access to her slowly growing moist flesh.

He pushed back from her wet mouth a second later, shoved her back down onto the couch and stood up. Muttering a protest, she opened her eyes to find him staring at her, his chest heaving, breathing heavy. She laughed aloud; her skirt bunched up around her hips and spread her bare legs wider so that one leg rested on the couch, the other on the floor.

Rubbing both hands across his face, he closed his eyes briefly and blew out a breath. Staring at her closely, he asked, "Do you know what the hell you are doing? I am so ready to fuck to you now, it is not funny. You better not be playing any game with me. If I were you, I would leave now while I still had a chance, because once I get a hold of you, I may not let you go for a long time. Oh yeah, and one more thing: this better not be a ploy to get pregnant either. Damn it, I am not even sure that I have any protection."

Looking up at him, she licked her lips slowly, drew her arms above her head and said, "I want your specialty, not your baby, so yes in answer to your question, I do know what the hell I am doing. I have protection in my purse, I came prepared. So the question is this though: What are you going to do about it?"

Not answering her question, he leaned over her and slowly placed both of his hands on her hips, gripped the sides of her panties and started to pull them down. "Put your legs together for a second, so that I can take these off or so help me I will rip them off of you," he instructed, leaning back to see if she would comply with his command.

She did indeed comply with his command and he slid the panties down her legs. She started to sit up then to remove her high heeled sandals as well, but he stopped her from doing so.

"Leave them on. Lay back and put both of your arms back up over your head," he said. After she did what he asked, he arranged her body so that one of her legs rested on the couch and the other rested on the floor. Moving between her splayed thighs, using his hands he placed his hands on the insides of her soft thighs and spread her even wider. She felt one minute of cool air sweep across her exposed flesh, before his fingers speared her curly black pubic hair open and his hot wet mouth covered her pink flesh.

Arching her back, her hips lifted up to welcome his wet invasion. She let out a moan, her dark brown eyes falling closed. His tongue licked across the top of her clitoris, then licked down to slide across the nub of flesh underneath. Then his lips closed around it. Drawing it between his lips, he began to suck on the tiny pink nub of flesh. One of his hands continued to grip one of her thighs to hold her open, while the index finger of his other hand slid into her. The walls of her vagina closed around his finger and, lifting his head for a second to look at her, he said, "Damn, but you are tight!"

Breathing heavily, she gasped, "Yesss...don't stop, please don't stop!"

He muttered, "Hmm..." into her curls and sucked harder onto her clit. She let out an unladylike groan and her hands came down to press his head into her aching, wet flesh.

He stopped once again, removed her hands from his head and looking up her, said, "Do you want for me to tie you up? I swear that's what I am going to do if you don't put your damn hands above your head like I asked."

Trembling, her breath ragged she put her hands back above her head like he told her to do so, gasping at the pillow behind her head. He was relentless then. His fingers, lips, tongue and even the slight brush of his teeth drove her crazy as he began to feast on her. She screamed, pleaded, swore as she trembled, her hips dancing but he gave her no relief. She came so many times that she lost count. Eyes watering, she pleaded with him to come inside of her, to fill her.

Finally, he took pity on her. He pulled away from her drenched passage and stood up. Looking down at her, his mouth shiny and wet from her essence, he said, "Undress for me."

She sat up, shaking slightly and pulled the shirt over her head, unfastened her bra. Tossing the items aside, she tilted her hips up and removed her skirt. With one leg on the floor and the other on the couch, she laid back spread eagle onto the couch. Looking up at him, she saw that he had pulled his shirt over his head and was working on removing his jeans. He finished undressing, then came back down over her body and lay down very carefully on top of her.

She sucked in a breath as she felt his chest press mash with her hard pointed nipples. He placed his legs in between her spread ones and, reaching up with both hands, he cupped her face in his hands. He stared at her for a minute. Then, just before covering her lips with his, he said, "Let me know if I hurt you at any time. I want to give you pleasure not, pain."

"I am fine. Kiss me, please," she said.

He complied with her plead and begin to kiss her, his tongue sweeping inside of her mouth, engaging her tongue in a duel with his. She moaned into his mouth, her neck having arched up to meet his wet mouth with hers; as her hands fell down to cup his butt. Tilting her hips upward, she started to wrap her legs around his back, but he stopped her.

Pulling back from her, he asked, "Wait; the condom. Where is the condom?"

Her eyes opened and she blinked for a second in an attempt to get her bearings, and then said, "In my purse, on the coffee table."

She watched as he opened her purse, pulled out a condom, and rolled it on. He started to lay back down over her, but dipped his head at the last minute to lave his tongue across each one of her hard pointed nipples. She groaned, arching her back. Her hands clasped his head to hold him to her. He let her hold his head to her chest for a second, and then he pulled away to blow gently on the hard tips. Half crazy with need, she reached out to him, her dark brown eyes pleading, "Please, you have to come inside me. I want to feel you inside me."

He took pity on her then and lay back down on top of her body, his legs once more moving in between hers. "Look at me; don't close those gorgeous dark brown eyes. I want you to know that it is me who is going to cum inside of you. I want you to know that it is me who is going to fill you, to fuck you."

He reached down and cupped her butt in both of his hands and pushed into her, hard. Gasping for breath, her hands grasped his shoulders as she felt his first hard thrust.

Leaning down to bite at her soft mouth, he said, "Wrap those caramel legs around me now."

She wrapped her legs around his waist as he had asked her to. He pulled slightly away from her then and thrust again, harder. Pulling away from his mouth, she screamed.

He pulled away, coming out of her completely and her eyes popped opened in confusion.

"What...?" She started to ask.

"Wait a second, I changed my mind. I want to go deeper; you are so tight. I want to feel you milking me, all of that tightness. Unwrap your legs from around me;

put them on my shoulders instead. Let's take the sexy heels off first, though."

He reached down and took the heels off of her feet, then came back to her. Placing her legs onto to his shoulders, he pushed back into her. This time when he pushed back into her, the force of his thrust made her slide on the couch. She screamed again, her back arching up, her hands reaching up to grasp at the arm of the couch. His hands reached up and covered hers, shoving his hard cock deeper into her drenched passage. It seemed like he wanted to brand her with his mark, as his possession.

She wasn't in any pain though. This is how she wanted it: to be dominated and stuffed to the core. Her vagina walls squeezed the length of his cock as he went even deeper into her, her tiny nub of flesh kissing it. He leaned down to kiss her and it was just enough to send her over the edge.

She came, moaning into his mouth, her tongue sliding across his. Pulling away from her, he rose to his knees, thrust one last time into her, held still and began to cum. He collapsed a few seconds later on top of her sweaty form and kissed the side of her neck, breathing deeply. She hugged him to her and kissed his shoulder, savoring the feel of his heavy form on top of her smaller stature. Getting his breath back, he reached up to kiss her lips, and then pulled away from her.

Standing up, he removed the used condom and tossed it into a nearby trashcan. Naked, he walked into the bathroom then. She laid on the couch for a minute then, her body tired and slightly achy, but fulfilled. A few seconds later, she sat up and began to dress back, forgoing the bra and panties. Gathering her underwear in one hand, she grabbed her purse in the other and slid the sandals back onto her feet. He had still not come out of the bathroom as she let herself out the front door.

As she slid into the car, she couldn't stop a moan from escaping her lips. She hurt. She would go home and take a hot shower to ease her pain from being thoroughly and utterly fucked out of her mind.

## *Taste Me*

I want to touch my "lips" to his beautiful mouth, to glide across his tongue and then beg of him to pause and hold me in his mouth for a second to savor the taste, and then allow my wetness to slide down his strong throat to satisfy his raging thirst...

And then, only then, I want for him to rise to his knees to draw the very tip of his cock down my clitoris one time, then place my legs upon his shoulders so that my toes point towards the sky and gently, oh so very gently, push his way inside of my dripping honey...

Greedy and achy with need, my hips will rise eagerly to meet his, as to not miss each and every single thrust...

And when we cum, it will be together, sweat dripping from our bodies, your name sighing from my lips as your warm essence shoots into my inner cavity, my muscles clamping around you to drain each and every drop...

### *Three Secrets*

She reached up, kissed her husband, Jesse, good-bye, and walked him to the door. Opening the front door to leave, he turned back around to say, "My flight should be in around 10am on Thursday morning. I am willing to take a taxi back home, but it would be even better if a certain someone would be there to greet me instead."

Gazing up into his dark, chocolate-brown eyes, she said, "Oh, you would, huh? We shall see, baby. I love you, take care."

He said, "Hmm...I wonder sometimes," laughed and leaned down to kiss her on the forehead. He then walked out the door.

Pulling back the pale blue curtain in the living room, she saw him climb into the taxi and watched as it pulled away from the curb.

As soon as the taxi disappeared from view, she pulled a cellular phone from the pocket of her blue chenille robe and punched in the familiar numbers. Smiling, she made an appointment for 9pm that night at Le Pavilion Hotel. Then, she placed the phone back in her pocket.

Turning on her heel, she climbed up the spiral staircase to ascend to the second floor. Walking into the master bedroom, she headed over to the closet and reached inside it for a red velvet-covered box. Opening the box, she removed the top shelf and, flipping a small switch; she reached into the second bottom compartment and pulled out some thin, yellowed pages. The pages, torn from the King James Version of the bible, were slightly frayed. Clasping the loose leafed pages, tied with a ribbon in one hand, she closed the box and replaced it back in its place inside the closet.

Walking inside the blue and gold bathroom, she placed the pages on the edge of the bubble bath filled tub and untied the belt of her robe. Before letting the robe fall away from her body, she took several hairpins and quickly pinned her hair up into a bun. Sinking into the warm bubbles, she untied the ribbon from the loose leaf pages and tossed the ribbon to the floor. Opening her hands, she let the loose leaf pages fall into the water. As she watched the pages from Acts 2:38 fall into the water, she whispered the following: "Forgive me father, for I am afraid that, once again, I am about to sin."

She stepped out of the tub forty-five minutes later and dried herself off with a huge yellow, fluffy towel. Walking towards the mirrored vanity, she removed a bottle of peach and papaya lotion from the top of it. Opening the bottle, she began to smooth the lotion across her nude flesh. After smoothing the lotion over her body, she lightly combed her scented fingers through the black curly thatch of hair at the top of her thighs. Reaching for the matching perfume, she sprayed her pulse points.

Then, still nude, she walked into the bedroom and opening the dresser drawer, pulled out a pair of satin coffee-colored panties. Sliding into them, she walked to the closet, pulled on a black sleeveless sundress, and slid her feet into a pair of high-heeled black sandals.

Walking back into the bathroom, she unpinned her hair, sprayed some hairspray on it, and then brushed the dark brown strands out straight. Quickly applying caramel foundation, black eyeliner and red lipstick, she walked back into the bedroom and reached onto the bed for the small black purse that rested there.

Five minutes later, after setting the house alarm, she drove out of the driveway, merged with the late-night traffic and headed for the La Pavilion. Driving into the garage, she parked, opened the glove box, and placed her wedding ring inside. She stepped out of the silver SUV, locked it, and then hurried to the service elevator. Stepping inside the elevator, she pressed the button for the 17th floor. Once the elevator stopped, she walked out into the main corridor and headed for the door at the end of the corridor. Pulling a key from her purse, she opened the door and stepped inside the cream-colored room.

A king-sized bed dominated one side of the room; a huge whirlpool tub dominated the other side. She knew that at the far end of the room was the bathroom, with a shower big enough to accommodate three people. The room also included a cream-colored couch that sat directly in front a flat screen television.

She slipped off her high sandals and placed her purse inside the bedside dresser. Tossing her hair over her shoulder, she hoped that the agency would grant her request at such a short notice. Although it had been a while since she had used their services, she knew that they usually tried their very best to please their clients.

She was in the middle of pouring herself a shot of vodka when she heard the door snap open. In nervous anticipation, she turned around and waited to see who the intruder or intruders were. Cameroon walked through the door first, followed by Antoine and Rick; all three were dressed in black suits. Lining up in front of the closed door, with their arms crossed over their chest, they stared at her for a second, not saying a word. Looking into their hazel, blue and light-brown eyes, she trembled slightly, and then placed the shot glass onto the wet bar and walked towards them.

Stopping in front of the three of them, she placed her hands behind her back and bowed her head to show them that she was ready to obey their commands.

Cupping her chin in his hand, Antoine was the first one to move forward. Smiling, he said, "Hello, baby girl. I have missed you. How have you been?" He hugged her close for a minute, and then stepped farther into the room. He picked up the remote for the television and went to take a seat on the cream-colored leather couch.

Rick stepped forward next, smiled at her and leaned down to place a quick kiss on her mouth. Walking over to the bed, he stripped down to his blue boxers and then went to sit on the edge of the king-sized bed.

Cameroon stepped forward last and placed a kiss on her forehead, stripped down to his blue boxers as well, then went to join Rick on the edge of the bed. Smiling at the three of them, she let out a laugh and, walking towards the bed, she said, "I believe that I am ready for a test ride."

Upon arriving at the edge of the bed, she stood placed her arms above her head, as Cameroon stood up to slip the sundress over her head. Tossing the dress aside, he pulled the covers from the bed and helped her onto the bed to lie flat on her back. Rick moved to the head of the bed and, cupping her chin in both hands, he began to kiss her. His lips moved over hers, his tongue driving deep inside of her hungry mouth, swirling inside to steal her breath away. Moaning into Rick's mouth, she felt Cameroon tying her hands together with a piece of rope. Rick pulled away from her mouth, took a hold of the rope in one hand and raised her hands above her head so that her back was arched up off of the bed. Licking her lips, she stared into Rick's blue eyes and said, "Please, kiss me again."

He laughed and then, cupping her chin with his other hand, he resumed kissing her.

Cameroon leaned over her body, cupped her breasts in both hands began to lave her nipples with his long tongue. Trembling slightly, she thrust her chest towards him, seeking his wet, warm mouth. Cameroon sucked each nipple in his mouth for a minute then licked his way down her body and spread her legs wide open with his hands. Moving down her body, he laid down on his stomach between her legs. Using his fingers, he speared her thatch of black curls open.

At the first lick of his long tongue, she jerked, her body bowing as she attempted to close her legs. But Cameroon used his shoulders to hold her legs open as he began to feast upon her, kissing and sucking the pink nub of flesh between her furry thatch.

Rick pulled away from her mouth and began to knead her tits with one hand, pinching and pulling at her swollen nipples. Rick watched her, his blue eyes hooded as her body arch up, chest lifting, legs falling open as she hissed in breaths of air, struggling to breathe.

Cameroon cupped her behind in both hands and stuck his tongue deep inside of her. She screamed just once before Rick clamped his mouth over hers; his mouth and tongue capturing her muffled moans of satisfaction. Cameroon stayed with her the entire time through her climax, drinking from her wetness. Then he placed a gentle kiss upon her turf of wet curls.

The two men then rose from the bed and arranged her body so that she lay on her back across the short end of the bed. Her head hung halfway off the bed on one end, her legs hung off the other way. Cameroon took off his boxers, sat down on a nearby chair that he had placed near the bed, and slid in between her spread thighs. He wrapped her legs around his waist and reared up inside of her, stuffing his penis deep; almost to the root.

Rick stripped out of his boxers, leaned over her face to cup her chin with one hand, and urged her mouth open so that he could place his swollen penis inside. Her lips and tongue closed around his penis as he began to slowly drive his penis deeper and deeper.

Gently rubbing her throat and chin, he whispered to her, "Suck it. That's right; you remember how to do it." He began to rock against her, fucking her mouth.

Tears drifted from her eyes as his swollen member seemed to almost hit the back of her throat.

Cameroon thrust in a rhythmic motion, coming out of the chair and cupping her behind with both hands. The sensations were incredible; one penis caused her some pain, while the other gave her pleasure. Overloaded with so much cock meat, her body could only take so much. It was only a few minutes later when she begin to shake, her muscles clamping down on Cameroon's penis as her climax overcame her. Cameroon went still, arched his back, and then shot his load inside of her filling her with his warm cum.

Rick came inside of her mouth at the same time, his slightly salty cum shooting down her throat, both hands grasping her chin. Rick pulled his slack penis from her mouth, slipped on his boxers, kissed her on the forehead and then walked into the bathroom.

Cameroon helped her sit up on the edge of the bed and untied the rope from around her wrists. He then rose to his feet, slipped on his boxers and walked over to the tub to fill it up.

She slowly stood to her feet and walked into the bathroom to join Rick.

"Are you okay?" He asked, his blue eyes staring at her. "Cameroon and I weren't exactly gentle with you this time, but it has been awhile."

Picking up a toothbrush and paste from the vanity, she said, "No, baby, I will be okay. I have missed you guys as well."

"Good," Rick said, gently tapping her on the butt. Then he turned to walk back out of the bathroom.

She brushed her teeth, wiped her mouth with a towel, and then walked back out into the main room. Cameroon and Rick were sitting on the couch watching television when she walked out; Antoine was sitting inside the whirlpool tub. He smiled at her as she walked towards him and slid inside the sudsy bubbles. Cupping the back of her head in one hand, he pulled her towards him and kissed her. Wrapping her arms around his head, she French-kissed him for several moments, then turned her back to him and sank to her knees before him. Antoine grabbed a hold of her hips and pulled her down onto his thick, swollen penis. She gasped as he began to thrust up inside of her still-swollen passage. Her tits bounced in the sudsy bubbles, as she arched her back against him, relishing the feel of having him inside of her once again. She let out a moan a few minutes later when he wrapped one hand in her hair and pulled her head back to graze his teeth along her neck. Reaching behind her, she wrapped an arm around his neck and began to kiss him. Antoine wrapped one arm around her body and began to finger her clit, thrusting ever deeper into her. He swallowed her moan with his mouth, moved his hand up to cup one of her tits in his hands and pulled at the pointed nipple.

She broke away from his mouth. Trembling and arching her back as she began to climax. Her muscles clamped around Antoine and he reacted by going still, then shooting a load of cum into her drenched passage. Antoine stepped out of the whirlpool tub a few minutes later and dried himself off with a big, fluffy, cream-colored towel. He then helped her out of the tub and Cameroon came over to dry her off with a matching towel.

Cameroon moved the towel gently between her legs, then placed a soothing gel between her swollen lips. He took her hand and sat down in a chair, placing her in front of him, urging her to step upon a small step stool. She knew what was coming and her breath caught in anticipation; the three of them had done something similar to this before.

She was about to be serviced by Cameroon, Antoine and Rick all at the same time. Each of her secret places would be fondled, caressed, licked and kissed. She leaned forward and clasped the back of the chair that Cameroon sat in and spread her legs, sticking out her behind.

Rick walked up behind the chair and, cupping her face in both hands he began to kiss her, his lips moving on her, driving and swirling his tongue inside of her hungry mouth.

Antoine moved behind her body, grasped her hips, and sank into her from behind. Cameroon licked her tits that hung in front of his face, while driving his fingers deep inside of her, rubbing her G-spot with one big finger.

She was glad that the three of them supported her body; otherwise, she was afraid that her legs would have given out from beneath her. Her body rocked back and forth, as she followed the movement of Cameroon's finger forward and then pushed back against Antoine to meet his driving penis. Rick swallowed her moans with his mouth as lights flashed behind her closed eyelids.

A few minutes later, the sensations became too much and, arching her back, she pulled her mouth from Rick's and screamed. She almost blacked out as the force of her climax hit her, vaguely feeling Antoine shooting his load between the fleshy cheeks of her behind.

Cameroon caught her body as her legs gave out and she fell forward. Cameroon lifted her up in his arms, laid her dripping, sweaty body onto the bed and placed one more kiss upon her mound. He then rose to his feet, but not before placing the covers over her. Sleepily, she looked up at the three of them standing beside the bed and said, "You guys are something else. No doubt, I will be sore tomorrow, but I had a really good time. Until next time."

The three of them laughed and said together, "We enjoyed you, as well."

Winking at her with his gorgeous hazel eyes, Cameroon said, "I aim to please." He waved her panties in front of her face. "I am keeping these."

Antoine gave her a sexy grin, his light brown eyes twinkling and said, "It is simple baby girl, your clit loves my dick."

Rick shook his head; his hooded blue eyes looked sleepy as well, as he placed a kiss upon her hair, saying, "You are crazy."

She snuggled down into the covers and watched the three of them dress and leave the hotel room. She fell promptly fast asleep with a wide smile on her caramel colored face.

The next morning, after having freshly showered and dressed back into her black sundress and sandals, she sat down to eat a breakfast of three medium pancakes, two scrambled eggs, and orange juice. She was ravenous, but then she always was after have been visited by her own special ordered CAR.

An hour later, she wrapped her arms around Jesse and kissed him passionately. She loved being visited by CAR occasionally, but she sincerely loved her husband. She loved everything about him; his keen sense of intelligence, his quiet strength and the safety he offered her. Jesse kissed her back, slung his overnight bag over his shoulder and wrapped an arm around her waist. Then the two of them walked out of the airport into the sunshine.

# I Once Had a Lover

I once had a lover, who had eyes the color of coffee and lips sweeter than the sweetest toffee

I once had a lover, who had eyes as mysterious as night and he used to love me until the morning light

I once had a lover, who had eyes of the steeliest silver and one look at him could all but make me quiver

I once had a lover, who had eyes the color of grass and such a fine ass

I once had a lover, who had eyes the color of the sky and the things he did to me, well made me want to holler and fly

But, one thing I can say is that all my lovers really knew how to love me and that's definitely no lie

# Hazel Eyes

I drove down the dark lonely road that night, with the radio on as my only companion. With my high beam headlights on, I peered through the darkness, on the alert for any deer that may decide to cross my path. It had been six months since I had last drove this road and I did not want to miss my turn off.

I had been driving for about twenty minutes or so when Marvin Gaye's song, "Sexual Healing" came onto the radio. I turned the volume up and began to sing along with the song, a wide smile on my face. I laughed aloud with delight, knowing that was exactly what I was going to get tonight and then some. The initial nervousness that I had experienced six months ago, the first time, was no longer there. I was a woman on the prowl. I wanted to be fucked by a certain hazel-eyed guy and I was going to get my chance tonight.

It was about fifteen minutes later when I pulled into his driveway and turned the car off. Scooping up my cellular phone with one hand, I grabbed my keys with the other. I locked the car doors, walked up the steps, and opened the door to let myself in. I headed for the bedroom, toed my slippers off upon reaching it, and dropped my cellular phone and keys by the slippers onto the floor.

I looked around for him; I glanced towards the bed but did not see him. Turning around, I headed back towards the kitchen where two cats greeted me. I reached down to stroke the top of Grace's head, the black and white one. The other cat, that I did not recognize, was gray and white in color. It stalked away from me when I reached out a hand to it. Head down, stroking Grace's soft fur, I said to the top of her head, "Hey girl, where are your owners at?"

Just then something told me to look up. I did and suddenly he was standing there, right in front of me. Wearing only a greenish colored towel wrapped around his waist, he looked at me and said, "You scared the shit out of me."

Damn, I thought to myself, he looks good enough to eat. I had never had a man greet me wearing only a towel. He never failed to surprise me; I think that is why I always came back to him. The first night he had fucked me, he wanted me to spend the night and, when I refused, he stole my underwear in retaliation. But not before eating me out while I sat on his face, his huge hands cupping my ass to prevent me from wiggling away.

Giving him a smile, I replied, "That's what you get for always leaving your front door open all of the time. Where did the other cat come from? I don't remember seeing her the last time I was here."

Walking past me, he replied over his shoulder, "That's my cat, Fluffy and you better not hurt her, either."

I said, "Whatever!" Rolling my eyes at his retreating back, I followed him back into the bedroom.

Upon reaching the bedroom, he sat down on the edge of the bed and began to fiddle with his computer for a second. I walked towards the other side of the room and started to reach down to pick up my cellular phone from the floor.

He looked away from the computer and said, "Come here woman."

"No," I said. "I am not 'coming' anywhere. You said that you had a lot of work to do, so I am not going to bother you. I just came to keep you company and to avoid getting on your nerves."

He let out a loud sigh, removed his eyeglasses and repeated once again, "I said come here, woman."

I dropped the phone and walked over to the bed, sitting down close beside him, so that my soft white cotton pajama leg was pressed up against his bare hairy leg. Looking at him, I said, "I am here. So what are you going to do now?"

He murmured "Hmm…" Then as if on one accord, we moved our faces closer together and our lips met. We kissed for a minute or two, and then rubbed noses for a couple of seconds, staring into each other's eyes. My dark-brown gaze clashed with his hazel gaze for a minute, than I wrapped my arms around his neck, sinking my hands into his short, dark-brown, slightly-wavy hair. I then pulled him down with me to lie back onto the bed.

Leaning over me, he kissed me deeper this time, his tongue driving deep into my greedy mouth, seeking the gum that rested inside. He pulled away and sat up when he realized that I was not going to let him steal my gum willingly this time. We have been playing this little game between the two of us for some time now and it never ceased to arouse me. Every time that I kissed him, he would steal the gum from out of my mouth with his tongue.

The first time that he did this to me, I admit that I was totally grossed out, but he has since taught me to enjoy this form of foreplay, this intimacy. That is why I took pity on him (and myself), but not before giving him a mischievous, teasing smile. Then, I moved the gum towards the front of my mouth to let it rest lightly between my teeth.

He didn't say anything but rolled his gorgeous hazel eyes at me.  Reaching down to me he removed the gum from between my lips with two big fingers. He leaned back down over my body and resumed kissing me then. He tasted so damn good, even better then last time. I think that it was because he had not smoked a cigarette beforehand. I loved kissing him, but sometimes it got on my nerves if I tasted tobacco on his lips, instead of just his own special taste.

Still kissing me, his hands roamed over my body, one hand reaching down to delve inside my white cotton pajama bottoms. Sliding his hand into my satin black panties, he stroked his fingers through my curly black pubic curls and shoved one finger inside of my tight pussy. I moaned into his mouth and spread my legs wider, tilting my hips so that he could have easier access to my aching flesh. He pulled away from my wet mouth and I muttered a protest until I felt his hand sliding under my blue tank top to push my black bra up.

Gaining access to my left nipple, he latched onto the pointed nipple and drew it into his mouth, suckling it. I was assaulted by double sensations then as one big finger moved deeper inside of me and a wet mouth sucked and laved my tit. One of my hands reached down to hold his dark head to me, while the other one held onto his arm, my body arching up to meet his invasion.

He sat up suddenly and, shoving both hands into my panties, he pulled both my panties and pajama bottoms off at the same time. I started to pull my tank over my head and was in the process of unfastening my bra when he lost his towel and moved between my legs. Spreading them wide, he moved between them and thrust inside of me. Arching my back up, arms over my head, tangled in my tank top, I groaned and started to wrap my legs around his hips.

Staring down at me, he said, "No, keep them legs open wider."

I felt invaded, stretched, when he first came inside of me, but my body quickly adjusted to his hard, thrusting penis. Biting my bottom lip, I lifted my hips up to meet his; I wanted him to go deeper. I wanted to know that he had been there even hours after we finished.

Staring into his gorgeous, slightly-slanted hazel eyes, I said, "Deeper. Please, you have to go deeper."

Placing my legs over his shoulders, so that my legs were in the shape of a "v", he leaned over me and shoved himself deeper into me. Shoving his hands into my hair, he leaned down further and gave me his tongue; I opened my mouth to take it. My lips sucked on his tongue as the walls of my vagina sucked on his cock. Dual sensations, wetness against wetness; I was in ecstasy.

Pulling away from my protesting mouth a few minutes later, his mouth shiny from my kisses, he said, "Cum for me."

"I can't," I said, frightened of losing control.

"Yes, you can," he said. Then he grabbed my hips with both hands and, arching his back, began to cum inside of me, drenching me with his warm essence. He pulled out of me a second later and helped me removed the tank and bra. Then, spreading my legs wide apart, he began to eat me out.

"Please don't!" I said, trying to pull his head away.

He murmured, "No!" into my black pubic curls and his mouth began to suck on my clit.

## *Caress Me Inside*

As she tied the silk kimono belt to her matching robe around her waist, she thought to herself, What the hell am I getting myself into? Yeah, she had done this before, but how many years ago had it been? 8? 9? Yes, she had been naked then, too, but a woman had done it and she had enjoyed it. A woman's hands and fingers had touched her bare skin, smoothed across her shoulders. Though the woman had not come to her house and invaded her personal space. The setting had been controlled then, but this time... well the situation would be different.

Nobody would monitor what went on behind these walls. There would be nobody to question or answer to. Anything and everything could happen tonight and nobody would have to know. Sweeping a hand across her dark brown hair, she threw her head back and laughed. Oh yes, tonight she would embark on an experience to remember; an experience that would allow her to be sensuous, uninhibited and free. Free from restrictions, free to explore, free to drown in touch. She could not wait.

The doorbell rang just then and her pink toes carried her towards her dynasty.

Peeking through the peephole, she licked her full, shiny, red lips at the sight of him. Her nervous fingers slid across the lock for a second, than she opened the door and took a step back to allow him entrance. He stepped inside, closing the door behind himself and she took a breath, inhaling the scent of pure man. The combination of aftershave and cologne teased at her senses. Damn! He both smelled and looked good.

Dark haired with blue piercing eyes, he stood about six feet tall. He was dressed in a white tee-shirt, a pair of khakis and a pair of black leather sandals. In one hand, he carried a long black case; on one shoulder a black gym bag. Smiling at her, he extended his hand to her.

"Hello," he said. "I'm Bryan. You must be Rachel."

Rachel placed her right hand in his and nodded her head.

A second later, he pulled his hand away to say, "So, Rachel, where can I set up at?"

"You can set up in here. Besides the bedroom, this is the biggest room in the house. Do what you have to do and let me know when you are ready. May I get you something to drink, perhaps?" Rachel asked.

"Sure," he said. "Iced water, please."

"A glass of iced water it is then," Rachel said.

Rachel turned and walked to the kitchen to get the requested drink. When she returned, Bryan had set up a low, black-padded table in the middle of the room. A white, thin sheet covered the surface, and a small white pillow lay at one end while a pile of white towels lay at the other end. A foldable small dressing screen was set up in one corner of the room, while soft flute music played from the stereo. Bryan took the tall, cold glass of iced water from her outstretched hand and smiled down at her.

"Thanks," he said. "You can disrobe behind the dressing screen; I took the liberty of turning up the thermostat up a notch, too. You can wrap yourself in one of the bigger towels. I don't want you catching a cold on my watch."

Rachel took the offered towel, laughing and said, "Thanks for being so considerate."

She went behind the screen, untied her belt and let the gown drop to the floor. Wrapping the fluffy white towel around her body, she stepped out from behind the screen and walked towards the table. Before lying down upon the table she opened the towel and lay naked upon it, letting the towel drape loosely over her body. Turning her face to the side, she laid her head down upon her crossed arms which rested on the pillow.

Bryan moved to the front of the table, right above her head then. Rubbing his hands together to warm the oil between them, he leaned over and whispered in her ear, "Relax and enjoy."

Sliding the towel down to her waist, he leaned over and smoothed his hands up her back. Sweeping his hands over her shoulder blades, he began to massage the oil into her sore muscles. Bryan massaged her back and shoulders for a few minutes, then stopped and moved to her left side.

Rachel muttered, "Why did you stop? That felt so good. Pilates class kicked my butt today."

Bryan laughed and said, "Glad that you have enjoyed it so far. Relax, I plan on continuing on; I aim to please. Lay your head flat on the pillow and stretch both of your arms out." Bryan instructed her.

Rachel did as he asked and Bryan smoothed the oil over both of her arms. Then, cupping her much smaller hands in his, he massaged her hands, his fingers smoothing through hers. Moving to the end of the table to stand at her feet, he started to rub oil onto her feet, paying extra special attention to each individual toe. When Bryan smoothed his fingers around her little toe, Rachel couldn't help herself; a giggle escaped from her lips.

"Ticklish, eh?" Bryan said, "Hmm...I wonder where else you are ticklish at?"

Feeling very relaxed and somewhat sleepy, Rachel said, "Wouldn't you like to know?"

"I will find out if you are ticklish anywhere else on your body, you can count on it. Is it okay if I remove the towel completely now? Are you comfortable? Warm enough yet? The reason why I am asking is because it will be much easier to do your legs then." He explained.

Not even bothering to lift her head from the table, she murmured, "Sure, I am warm enough. Go for it."

Bryan removed the towel and smoothed his oily hands up her right leg, his fingers gently caressing the sensitive skin at the back of her knee. He stopped at the very top of her thigh, just before the swell of her right buttock and proceeded to repeat her left leg to the same treatment. After carefully rubbing the oil into the flesh of her left thigh, he settled both of his hands onto the twin cheeks of her butt.

Rachel couldn't help herself, although she had expected it, it still felt strange when he touched her bare behind; involuntarily her body tensed up. He felt it almost immediately and he went still, asking, "Are you okay? I don't want to make you uncomfortable. Do you want me to stop?"

She paused for half a second, and then said, "No, I am okay. I don't know what came over me. Keep on going. We are both adults here, after all."

"Okay," Bryan said. "But stop me at any time if I make you uncomfortable." He then began to massage the twin moons gently, but when he ran one finger along the crease in between, Rachel found herself sucking in a breath.

"Okay?" he asked, his hands going still on her bare flesh.

"Okay," she murmured back to him, but it was not okay by all means. Embarrassed beyond belief, but unable to help herself, Rachel had found herself becoming wet the moment he had smoothed his hands across her butt. When he had run his finger along the crease, she had wanted to spread her thighs, tilt her butt up in the air and beg for more; it had felt so good.

Bryan ran a finger along the crease one more time, and then asked her to turn over onto her back. Face flushed, she kept her eyes closed tightly as she turned over onto her back like he had asked her to do so. He laughed aloud when he saw her telltale hard nipples, knowing immediately that she had been aroused by his ministrations.

Eyes still closed, she said, "I am so embarrassed. Please, stop laughing; it is not funny."

He stopped laughing at once and said, "Stop worrying. It's okay really; at least now I know that you have enjoyed yourself so far. Your aroused body is proof that you are relaxed, comfortable. Shall I continue?"

"Yes," she said arms at her sides, her body tense and legs pressed closed tightly together. Eyes still closed she breathed in and out, willing her torturous nipples to go away.

He continued on with his massage then, smoothing his oily hands around her neck, across her shoulders and down her arms. When he settled his hands just above her belly button, he said, "Open your eyes and watch the curves of your body respond to the touch of my hands. Experience, savor the whole delicious effect and, damn it, relax your body. You are so darn tense. I don't bite unless asked to do so."

Her tongue came out and licked dry lips. She slowly opened her eyes to find him staring directly at her. His blue eyes held hers as he moved his hands up slowly until they cupped a tit in each hand. Her legs opened up slightly and she arched her back slightly, so that her tits filled his hands to overflowing. They watched each other as his hands weighted her for a minute, then his thumbs smoothed over her hard, pointed nipples. She hissed in a breath, as her legs moved restlessly on the table.

"Hmm…" he said. "Do you want me to touch somewhere else? It is only the two of us here; nobody has to know. Tell me what you want, what you need."

Beyond caring anymore, Rachel gasped out, "Please…touch me between my legs."

"Your wish is my command," he said and moved to the end of the table. Cupping her feet in both of his hands, he said, "Relax your legs and spread your knees."

Rachel did as he asked and his hands rubbed both of her feet, rubbing gently in between each individual toe. Closing her eyes once more, she relaxed as her body grew warm from his sensual touch.

Bryan smoothed his hands up the insides of her legs. When he reached her thighs, he spread them wide with his hands. Pausing, he said, "Open your eyes. Watch me."

Rachel opened her eyes like he asked her to and he began to move his hands once more. Breathing through her parted lips, she watched as he reached the top of her thighs and combed his fingers through her nest of curls. Combing through the warm wetness, he carefully spread her clitoris open and then lowered his dark head. Rachel's stomach caved in as soon as she felt the first slow lick of his tongue, her palms falling to rest upon his shoulders.

Bryan speared one finger, and then two sank deep into her wetness, while his tongue teased at her pink flesh. Rachel tilted her hips up towards his mouth, determined to feel every lick, every nip of his teeth. Burying her hands into his dark strands, she held his head to her moist flesh. She started to see stars behind her closed eyelids and a second or two later, she came hard, shaking. He stayed with her the entire time, sucking her wetness up into his mouth, fingers soothing her trembling. A minute later, when she opened her eyes, she found him staring at her smiling.

"Welcome back," he said, his blue eyes twinkling. "You are so responsive, I love it!"

Legs still spread wide, she said, "That was...I have no words." Then she looked down at his bulging crotch. "I would love to feel you inside me, though."

He laughed and said, "I would love that too. Hold on a second while I get some protection." He pulled his shirt over his head and unzipped his pants in a matter of seconds. He was nude under his slacks and, after pulling on a condom, he moved between her legs and cupped her behind in his hands. "Slide up a bit for me, to the edge of the table," he said. "I want to get inside of you real good."

Rachel did as he asked and a second later he shoved inside of her, sinking deep. Grasping his forearms, her body arched up off the table, she screamed.

Pulling out of her partway, he placed her legs in a "v" against his shoulders and his hips began to move. His hands held her legs to his chest as he stuffed his swollen, hard cock into her.

Hips still moving, he looked down at her and said, "Fold your arms behind your head so that I can have a full view of your tits. I want to see them move as I stuff myself into you. Keep your eyes open, though; I want us to watch each other as we cum."

Rachel did as he asked and he began to move faster. Their pubic hair mashed together as he worked himself deeper into her drenched opening. Eyes watering, but still open, her legs tensed against his chest as she started to climax a few seconds later. His hips went still a second or two later as he came as well, his blue eyes blazing into her dark-brown ones.

## Remember Me

"I want you to remember me," she said, giving him a wicked little grin before she proceeded to speak again. "Watch my tongue as I draw this lollipop into my mouth. See my cheeks clench as I suck the sweet treat, lips moist around the head. Do you want a taste? You do, don't you? No, not just yet!"

Laughing softly, she pulled the lollipop out of her mouth to say, "Let me make it a little bit wetter for you."

She returned the treat once more between cherry red lips. Then holding his gaze the entire time, she reached under her skirt and, wiggling her generous hips, proceeded to remove her powder blue lace panties. She stepped out of them and spreading her legs, bent her knees slightly.

His breathing had changed, she noticed, and his face was somewhat flushed as he realized what she was about to do.

Bending her head, she removed the lollipop from her mouth and slowly, painstakingly dragged the cherry flavored tootsie roll pop down her clitoris once, then twice.

He let out a groan and reached for her, but she giggled and stepped just out of his reach.

"Oh, no, my love," she said, holding the candy out to him. "You cannot have me; instead, enjoy this sweet, wet treat and remember me."

Frustrated and hard with need, he took the offered treat from her hand. Before placing the lollipop into his mouth he said, "Damn girl, you really know how to bring a man to his knees."

"Well, then," she said with a wide grin, "I better leave while you can still stand."

She then reached down to scoop up her panties, turned around and ran.

## *Open up Wide*

"Come on," he said. "Hop on."

She swallowed and wiped her sweaty palms down her pants legs. Then she reached for his hand and, mimicking his earlier actions, got on. The bike rocked and she trembled.

"Whoa," he said as he spread his feet farther apart on the ground. "Steady now. Relax." He took her hands and placed her arms around his waist. Flushed up against his back, she savored the feel of his hard back against her softer front. Turning his head slightly he said, "Ready? Oh yeah, one more thing: When we reach a curve, lean with me and try to keep talk to a bare minimum. Bugs are out in full force this time of year. Okay?"

"Okay," she said. "Ready."

A few minutes later, they peeled out of the parking lot and roared off. The ride was cold and fast;

she savored every movement of it. Colors and lights zoomed by. All too soon, they pulled to a stop into an apartment complex. Pulling into a parking space, he cut the engine and got off the motorcycle.

"Come on," he said, holding the handlebars with both hands to steady it.

She swung one leg over to get off and almost stumbled. He steadied her for a minute with his hands on her waist, and then stepped back. Reaching up to unfasten her helmet, he took his off too, laughed and said, "You can tell that you have never had one of these between your legs before."

"No, I have not had anything like it between my legs before," she could not help but agree. The sexual innuendo was not lost on her, but she was far from being offended. Walking along behind him, she followed him up two flights of stairs before he stopped in front of a door. He opened the door and motioned her inside ahead of him. Flicking the light switch, he hung his coat up and did the same with hers. Toeing his shoes and socks off, he placed his helmet on a sidebar and did the same with hers.

"Let me change clothes," he said and turned to walk on through the apartment to a back bedroom. Returning a few minutes later, he was barefoot and dressed in a tee-shirt and baggy brown shorts.

Turning into a small kitchen, he said, "Make yourself at home."

"Thanks," she said, removing her sandals before she walked into the living room.

"Have you eaten?" He asked as he prepared dinner.

She said, "I am fine. No, but thanks; I am not hungry."

"Want a beer?" he asked.

"No not really. I will take water instead," she replied.

Wandering over to the balcony glass doors, she paused before opening them and asked, "May I?"

"Help yourself," he replied.

Opening the doors and crossing to the railing, she breathed in the heavy summer night for a few moments. A couple of minutes later, he joined her on the balcony, carrying a bottle of beer and a glass of water in one hand and a plate in the other. She walked to him, took the glass of water, and sat down to join him at the table.

He ate in silence for a minute, then he said, "Are you sure that you do not want any? It is my secret recipe."

"I am not hungry," she repeated with a small smile, "But I will taste it, okay?"

He held a forkful up to her mouth with a grin. Holding his gaze, she opened her mouth and accepted his offering. She chewed, swallowed and then said, "Not bad."

"I know," he said, looking smug. "You know it tastes better being washed down with some beer."

"Okay," she said with a sigh and a grin. "I do not like beer, but I will drink it this once because you asked me to do so."

He handed her the bottle and saying, "Damn, you are too easy; I wonder what else you will do if I asked it of you?"

After taking a small sip of his beer, she handed the bottle back to him. Staring into his eyes, she said, "Why don't you find out?"

Pushing his now-clean plate and empty beer bottle aside, he said, "Come here."

He scooted his chair back from the table. She rose from her chair and, staring into his eyes, walked around the table to him. Taking her hand, he pulled her around to the front of his body, between his now splayed legs. He tugged her down until she ended up on her knees. Between his legs, and eye level to him now, she splayed her hands on his chest and stared into his eyes. Grabbing a handful of her braided hair with one hand, he pulled her head towards him. The other hand cupped her neck, then smoothed across her shoulder; his fingers occasionally sliding under her top to fiddle with her bra strap. Leaning into her, he placed his mouth on hers and began to bite at her lips. Sliding his tongue deep into her mouth, he began to entice her with his ravage kiss. He tasted of beer, spicy chicken and pure hot man. He kissed her hungrily, sucking her tongue, and then giving his to her. Just when she was starting to feel lightheaded, he broke away from her wet mouth and leaned down to take a bite out of her neck. Slowly opening her eyes and breathing hard, she could not stop the gasp of pain from the sting.

He pulled her head back with both hands and said, staring at her, "I am not a gentle, patient man. I like everything I do to be rough and fast."

"I know," she whispered, licking her already wet lips.

"Will you really do anything I want?" He asked, still staring into her eyes.

"Yes," she said, sinking into the whiskey depth of his eyes.

"Okay," he said. Leaning back into his chair, he pulled the tee-shirt over his head. Tossing it aside, he said, "Finish undressing me."

Looking around her nervously, she started to say, "But...someone might see..."

Sighing, he started to stand. He pushed her aside, saying, "I figured as much; still the same scared mouse you were before. Are you afraid that mommy and daddy might not approve? Shit, some things never change.

You are a damn tease. It is so dark out here and nobody can see a damn thing, unless they had a spotlight on us." His eyes cruelly hardened.

"No...stop, please," she protested, grasping at the loop holds of his shorts with both hands when he made a move to stand. "I am just a bit embarrassed. I am not that experienced at this, that is all."

Relaxing once again back into his chair, he narrowed his gaze. Staring at her, he said, "Just what do you mean about not being that experienced? I don't do virgins, little girl. You can go play somewhere else if that is the case."

"I mean just not experienced in that aspect," she said blushing. "I haven't engaged in that much oral sex; that's what I meant." She licked her lips. Okay, how did this month's Cosmo describe how to do oral sex? She struggled in vain to think.

"That's okay," he said. "I will teach you how I like it."

He placed a quick open-mouthed kiss on her lips and then he said once again, "Finish undressing me."

She took a breath and proceeded to draw his zipper down. Shifting his hips, he let her pull the shorts down around his ankles. With her gaze still on his ankles, she said, "Step out of them."

He shifted his feet out of them, then leaned back and waited. Sliding her gaze back up, she could not prevent a gasp from escaping her mouth, for he had been naked under his shorts.

Laughing, he said, "You are acting as if you haven't seen a grown man's cock before. Who the hell have you been fucking all these years? Just immature boys?"

His manhood rested between a nest of reddish brown curls, long and slightly erect. Grabbing a hold of her braids with both hands, he pulled her head towards it. Taking her cool hands in his, he placed his hands over hers and began to show her how to touch him; gently in some spots, harder in other spots. His cock began to swell a few seconds later as she put her hands and fingers to work.

Breathing heavily, he managed to say, "Okay, now your mouth; I want your mouth on me."

She moved her head to comply and slowly licked the slightly wet head. Holding her head with both hands, he said, "Take me in your mouth and suck."

"Harder!" He said when she started to suck him slowly. Opening her mouth wider, she felt his hard cock at the back of her throat as she struggled to do as he asked. Maybe a minute or two later, he began to cum, gushing into her mouth. The salty essence filled her mouth to overflowing and, choking slightly, she started to pull her mouth away.

Opening his eyes and breathing hard, he said, "Swallow me, all of it!"

Sitting back on her haunches, holding his gaze, she did as he asked. The salty essence slowly slid down her throat and, although the taste was somewhat bitter, she held his gaze and swallowed.

Cupping her under the chin, he said, "Good girl!"

Staring into her eyes, he pulled away. He picked his shorts and shirt up in one hand and, still fully nude, turned to walk back into the apartment.

She sat there for a few seconds, still on her knees, her hands on her thighs, her head hung, breathing in and out. She had done it; finally stepped over the line. Now there was no way in hell of going back. He had her where he wanted her and she was a bit scared. Yet, that fear was not enough for her to run away from him. Therefore, after replacing her lip gloss, taking a sip of water and popping a mint into her mouth, she arose to her feet. Swaying slightly, she followed him back into the apartment.

He turned towards her, fully dressed, and handed her a helmet.

"Ready?" He asked.

Numbly, she nodded to him and turned to follow him out of the apartment. A few minutes later, they were on his motorcycle, weaving in and out of traffic, heading back to the store. About fifteen minutes later, they pulled to a stop beside her car and she slid off the bike from behind him and handed her helmet to him.

"Wait!" he said when she turned to go, and grabbed her right hand in his. Pulling her to him, he lifted his visor on his helmet and pressed a quick closemouthed kiss on her lips. "Give me a call sometime next week, I am listed. Go now." Before she could even leave the parking lot he had roared away, off into the night.

## Love Awake!

Strip the bed; throw the pillows to the floor

Open the window, turn out the light

Walk to the front of the house and unlock the door

Let the storm in; listen to the sounds of the night

Embrace the danger, ignore your fear

Remove the garments that clothe your body

Inhale deeply; scream if you must, but do not shed a

tear

Free your mind; do not give a damn about nobody

Express your inner feelings; do not let your sensuous

sexuality whither and die

The night belongs to you; invite that man inside

It is time for his body to make your un-awakened one

soar and fly

The Department of Transportation has issued you a
license, making your mouth water in anticipation of the
ride

All good things must come to an end and morning will
come

Just think, though: despite the fact that your legs will
be numb, you would have had a jolly old good time
getting some

## *The Phone Call*

"Come to me tonight," he said.

"I can't," she said.

"Why not?" he asked. "Do you have anything to do tonight?"

"Well, no, not really," she said with a soft laugh.

"Well then come on over tonight, I need you," he said.

"Why do you need me specifically?" she asked, "Isn't there anyone else?"

"No," he said vehemently. "I need you."

Twisting a lock of dark brown hair around her index finger, the phone cradled against her chin, she let out a soft sigh, and then said weakly, "But my legs are not shaved. I did not have a chance to shave my legs today."

"Don't worry about it," he said. "I will shave them for you and I have something better than shaving cream too. I can use whipped cream."

"Oh my goodness, whipped cream," she said in genuine shock, "That's hot! I mean I have never had a man offer to shave my legs for me either. I don't know, though."

"Come on," he cajoled. "I need you so bad. I will even buy you some chocolate and pick up some pina-colada mix, too. After a few drinks, you should be okay, right?"

She sighed, and then said, "Well to be honest, I am kind of tired of the toy. It has been a month for me. I haven't been kissed in a while either, I would love that. But you can't have a cigarette before kissing me, either. I don't want to taste tobacco on your lips."

"I will brush my teeth before I kiss you, I promise. It has been a while for me, too, a while since I had some," he said. "Come on over. I need you, I want you. Hell, if you were here right now, I would put you up on the table...and...I am starting to get hard right now just thinking about it."

"You are not, you cannot be getting hard, my goodness!" she gasped out loud, eyes closing briefly for a minute. Her hand gripped the phone tighter involuntarily. Opening her eyes a second later, she glanced down and sucked her bottom lip in between her front teeth.

"Oh no!" she moaned out into the phone.

"What do you mean, I can't be getting hard? I am horny, I need some so bad. You know how I feel about you. You were the one who made the rules and decided that we should just be friends in the first place," he said. "What is it, what's wrong?"

Before she could stop herself, she whispered into the phone, "You are not going to believe this, but my nipples have just gotten hard." Mortified after admitting this to him, she smacked a hand against her forehead, calling herself every type of fool for revealing that tidbit of information. Maybe he hadn't heard her, after all the fan was turned on high.

"What?" he asked. "I didn't hear what you just said."

"You heard me quite well, you liar," she said. "You just want me to repeat it again, but I won't."

Laughing in her ear, he said, "Yeah, I did hear you all right the first time. So your nipples are hard, eh? I aroused you, didn't I? You have to come to me now, so that I can help ease your misery. I have been dying to see those gorgeous big tits for a long time anyhow. Let's see...you are caramel colored, but your nipples are a little darker, aren't they?"

"Not funny, you dog," she said, mortified beyond belief. "How am I going to hide this when I walk out of the office? My clerks are going to see. As it is, they have been shooting me curious looks through the glass since I have been on the phone with you for about twenty minutes now. Damn you! You don't have to worry about anybody seeing you hard, because you are all alone."

He chuckled in her ear, and then said, "Well, what's your answer, ya or nay? What time do you get off, anyway? I get off here at ten; I'll be home around ten thirty. Don't deny me, please."

She said, "I get off at nine." She tapped her fingers on the desk in front of her for a minute, and then said, "Okay, I will come to you tonight. This is going to change things between us though, you know that?"

"I know things will change between us, we will become friends with benefits," he said, sounding quite pleased with himself. "So you are going to come? I can't wait."

"I am holding you to that offer to shave my legs, so don't try to wrangle your way out it. I am very intrigued now," she said mischievously. Then she said seriously, "Wait a minute, do you even have any protection? You know I am not on the pill now, the last thing I need is to end up pregnant with your baby. I have been told that I am quite tight too."

"Yeah, I got protection, KY jelly, and candles too. I remembered that you are not on the pill. You are a little hussy, you tease. Going to make me work for it, eh?" he said and roared with laughter for a minute.

"My word," she exclaimed. "You have thought of everything haven't you?"

Sobering he said, "Yes, I have. I know what I want, what I need. Okay, so well I will see you then, I promise you won't regret it."

The conversation ended then and she replaced the phone back into its cradle. Head down, sitting still for a minute afterwards, she began to breathe deeply. Silently, she willed her pointed nipples to go away. Lifting her eyes a second later, she glanced around quickly to see if any of her clerks were looking her way. Not seeing anyone staring directly at her, she tried to pull the white top away from her overheated body.

What had she been thinking, wearing a thin lacy white bra tonight? She should have known that he would do something like this; make her hot and horny, that is. He had called her twice before she had even left for work, leaving a voice message each time. She hadn't talked to him in several days and, all of a sudden, he had telephoned her out of the blue. Looking down at herself, she saw that the nipples were still hard. Her efforts had all been in vain, it seemed. Letting out a sigh, she decided to cross her arms across the undeniable evidence and make a beeline straight for the bathroom. With this thought in mind, she stood up, crossed her arms and opened the door.

"Ms...." one of her clerks said, walking towards her as soon as she opened the door. She quickly cut him off, "Excuse me, but I have to go to the little girls room. Talk to me after I get back, alright?"

"Okay," he said. "It can wait until you get back. Are you okay, Ms... you look a little flustered."

"I am fine, it's just so hot in here that's all," she said.

She hurried into the bathroom then. Once she was safely behind the locked steel door, she breathed out a sigh of relief. Looking into the mirror, she groaned aloud. Her clerk hadn't been lying; her cheeks were slightly red, a sheen of sweat shone shiny upon her forehead. Reaching behind her for the paper towel dispenser, she pulled a few out and wet them with cold water. Mopping her face with them, she willed her flushed cheeks to return to their natural caramel hue. Tossing them into the trash a few seconds later, she tore off a couple of toilet paper sheets from the roll.

Tearing them into several smaller sheets, she grimaced then lifted her top up to place them inside her bra, to cover her traitorous still hard nipples. Letting out a breath, she adjusted her top back into place and turned to the side to check out the view. Smiling in relief, she saw that the toilet paper had indeed served its intended purpose; the evidence had been covered up for now.

Before leaving the bathroom to return into the workroom, she glanced down at the Playboy bunny silver watch on her left wrist. Damn! She still had a whole hour and a half to go before quitting time. How in the hell was she supposed to last that long? She sighed, rolled her eyes, straightened her shoulders and opened the door.

Somehow she made it through the night, although more then once, her clerks had to repeat their questions to her. She was distracted, she admitted it, and if she were to be honest with herself a bit apprehensive too. She clocked out at nine o'clock that night and walked slowly towards the parking lot.

She knew that he had a view of her and she wondered if he watched her now. She longed to turn around to see if he had walked out onto the walk of the tower to get a better view of her. Feeling her heart skip a beat, she felt her panties began to go moist and willed herself not to turn around to steal a peek to check. Involuntarily, a moan uttered from her lips and she picked up her pace and walked a bit faster.

Reaching her car, she unlocked the door and dove inside, inside to safety for now. Putting the key into the ignition, she drove out of the parking lot like a bat out of hell. As she raced towards home, the warm night hair blowing her hair in the wind, she mentally calculated all that she needed to do before going to him tonight; Take a shower, brush teeth, pull hair back with an elastic band and hope that he decides not to run his fingers through it, replenish the supplies in her overnight bag, remove earrings (it might get a little rough). She

giggled at that last thought and sang aloud with the

radio to the tune of Sheryl Crow's song, "If It Makes

You Happy." Oh yeah, she was going to be bad tonight.

Let's see...hmmm...he would use regular shaving

cream to shave both legs quite naturally. But,

then....hmmm...whipped cream for the "V" between her

caramel thighs, perhaps strawberry flavored. Ah!

An hour and half later, she pulled her silver

Accent into his driveway. He must have been listening

for her because when she stepped out of the car, he

opened the screen door and stood on the front step. It

was still hot outside. The air was heavy with the scent

of rain as he stood on the top step and watched her

walk towards him. She had dressed in a Victoria Secrets

satin purple boxer set and a pink tank top. Underneath

the set, she wore a black satin bra set and her pink toes

were encased in a pair of high heeled sandals. Holding

his gaze with hers, she walked towards him with a

smile. Dressed in only a pair of jeans, with the top button unsnapped, he wore a blue towel slung around his neck.

"Hi," he said and reached for her left hand to help her up the steps. He led her inside then reached around her to shut the door with his other hand. Toeing off her high heels, she left them by the door.

When she pulled her hand from out of his, he said, "Hey, where are you going?" He pulled the towel from around his neck and looped it around her shoulders to pull her back towards him.

She laughed, removed the towel and said, "Relax, I was just going to put my bag down on the couch."

"Okay," he said, giving her a grin. "You look nice."

"Thanks," she said, giving him a shy smile.

"Want a drink?" he asked, moving towards the kitchen and tossing the towel onto the counter.

"Sure," she said and sat down on the couch.

A few minutes later, he walked back towards her, a tall frosty pina-colada drink in each hand, and a can of whipped cream under his arm.

He placed the whipped cream onto the coffee table and then handed her a drink and, in unison, the two of them took a sip of the cold liquid.

"Not bad," she said, sitting her glass down first onto the coffee table in front of her. Turning to him she licked her lips slowly and smiled at him.

"Glad you like it," he said, and then placed his drink down onto the coffee table beside hers.

"Well…" she said, still looking at him.

"Well, what?" He asked, reaching for her, one hand cupping the back of her neck and pulling her towards him. Holding her eyes with his, he leaned in closer to her and her dark brown eyes fell close as she realized that he meant to kiss her.

His lips settled onto hers and she sighed as she tasted the sweetness. The sweetness of the pina-colada on his lips, the brush of his tongue laving her bottom lip seeking entrance inside her mouth. Her lips parted granting him entrance and his tongue slipped inside her mouth, sliding against hers.

Their kisses became deeper a few minutes later, when she wrapped both arms around his neck and pulled him down with her to lie down on the couch. He settled down onto her body and tilted his head further to the side to ravage her soft mouth. She moaned into his mouth as she felt his harder, much larger frame sink onto hers. He kissed her a few minutes more, his tongue driving deep into her mouth. He pulled away from her wet mouth, a few seconds later though.

"What?" she said, still lying on the couch, eyes opening in confusion.

He said, "Wait a second."

She watched, eyes wide, as he picked up the can of strawberry whipped cream from the coffee table in front of him. Returning to her once more, he leaned down and ran his index finger along the seam of her lips, urging her to open the full lips. Holding his gaze with her own, she opened her mouth and nipped the tip of his finger. His nostrils flared, eyes going half closed at the teasing gesture.

"Close your mouth, you tease. You are going to pay for that," he said. She did as he asked, but not before giving him a teasing smile.

As soon as her lips closed he tipped the bottle and began to cover her lips with the pink gooey topping. Staring into her eyes the entire time, he lined her top lip first, then her fuller bottom lip. Moving back from her for a second to place the can back onto the coffee table, he then came back to sink down onto her body. Her tongue had just slipped out to steal a lick of the gooey mixture from her top lip, when he stopped her by cupping his hands around her chin.

"No," he said. "Don't, that's my treat, my dessert. Let me...lick you, taste you, wetness and all, bare flesh. Then I am going to rub against that tiny nub of flesh between your thighs and stuff myself deep inside of all that tightness. That's what I want to do all night. Will you let me, hmmm...?"

A moan escaped from between her lips as he painted the vivid picture of what he planned to do all her all night. Moisture began to gather between her legs and she longed to yank her panties off to feel his fingers, mouth, and cock driving into the wetness.

After propositioning her, without waiting for her reply, he leaned down and began to lick the whipped cream from her lips. He licked the top one first, and then slowly licked the bottom one. After licking both clean, he ran his long tongue along the seam of her lips to open them. Her mouth opened for his tongue, his lips and he kissed her again. Groaning into his mouth, her

back arched up and she wrapped her legs around his

waist. She shoved her hands into his hair to hold his

mouth to hers determined to taste every bit of the

sweetness of the pina-colada and the strawberry

whipped cream on his breath, lips, tongue.

### Price Check on Aisle 3

"Price check on aisle 3. Rachel from frozen foods, please dial register 5 for a price check."

Bent over at the waist, her head and upper body hanging inside of the freezer, Rachel vaguely heard her name being called for the second time on the loudspeaker. One palm lay flat on top of a box of chocolate fudgesicles, while her other palm rested on the top of a box of cotton candy popsicles. Legs spread and slightly bent, hips gripped almost painfully in Jonathan's gasp, her small sneaker clad feet lifted off of the floor with each thrust from his pounding hips. Jeans and panties around her ankles, Rachel was getting screwed out of her mind in a 24 hour grocery store, in plain view of everybody.

It had all happened so fast. Rachel had just started her shift for the night when Jonathan walked in. He had been drinking, she could tell; his eyes were slightly bloodshot. Upset, once again, from having been cheated on by his girlfriend, he had come to her for some advice. Having been friends with him for quite some time, she had seen him through many breakups over the years. After calming him down, she had given him her customary hug...when the hug became something else. Lifting her head from the middle of his chest with one hand, he had cupped her chin and just looked at her. Jonathan's green eyes had stared into her dark brown eyes for a couple of seconds, not saying anything until she wondered what was wrong with him. Finally, she asked, "What's wrong; why are you just staring at me?"

"It's nothing, no reason," he said. "Just, after all of these years, I realized just how sexy you are. Rachel, I..."

He had stopped in mid-sentence and had leaned down from his 6'2" height to crush his lips to hers. Shocked beyond belief, her dark brown eyes had gone wide the second his lips had touched hers. He tasted slightly of Jack Daniels and Coke, but Rachel tasted desperation more than anything. A minute or two later, her dark brown eyes fell closed, after admiring how long his blondish-brown eyelashes were, and she leaned up on her tiptoes to better enjoy the feel of his mouth against hers. The kiss became deeper then as her mouth fell open and his tongue had swirled inside to taste her. Jonathan cupped her face in both hands as his lean body bore her against the hard steel ice cream floor freezer. Rachel shoved her hands into his jeans back pockets and stretched her 5'1" ample frame upward to suck his bottom lip in between her soft full lips. Cursing under his breath, he had pulled away from her and both of his hands dropped to the zipper of her jeans.

Her eyes opening lazily, she had started to speak; but he shook his head at her, letting her know that no words were necessary. Dark brown eyes and green eyes locked then, as he unzipped her jeans and she, in turn, unzipped his. Reaching behind her, he shoved one of the sliding glass doors open, his green eyes smoldering, and said, "Turn around and bend over."

She turned around and bent over into the cold freezer as he asked her to do so.

"Lean down further," he ordered, one hand pressing the small of her back to help aide her. "Go up on your toes and brace yourself inside. I want to get inside of you, deep."

Rachel complied and then felt him pull down her jeans and pink panties. He had placed one small, wet kiss to her right buttock, before he began to drive his swollen cock inside of her. Gasping, her breath frosty, hands starting to grow cold, she let out a moan as he pushed his way inside her small opening. Jonathan hissed out a breath, gripped her hips harder and began to move, his cock driving deep.

The force of his thrusts lifted Rachel up, then down, as he filled her. She felt his pubic hair mash against the soft flesh of her buttocks as he changed the angle of his thrusts, as one hand came around and brushed through her tight black curls. When he stroked one finger through her wetness, it was just enough to send her over the edge. Rachel came then, pressing a box of chocolate fudgesicles against her mouth to muffle her scream of release. Jonathan thrust once more up inside of her, and then began to cum, filling her up. Rachel felt him pull out of her a few seconds later and heard him pull up his jeans. A minute later, she felt Jonathan pull her panties and jeans back up to cover her before walking away. She lay there in the freezer, still bent over, feet flat on the floor for a minute before she slowly rose to her feet.

"Rachel please report to the office immediately. Rachel from frozen foods, please report to the front office immediately," the loudspeaker sounded.

She began to laugh hysterically as she felt the wetness between her thighs, her hard nipples pressing against the lace of her bra. Zipping up her jeans, she straightened her blue smock over her white tee-shirt and went to face Mr. Branson's wrath. She was about to get fired no doubt, the store cameras had picked up her discretion and she didn't even really give a damn.

# Taste of Chocolate

Eyes glued to her mouth, he asked, "May I please have a taste?" The tone of his voice was pleading. "Why are you being so difficult about this? I know that your mamma taught you better. I know that she taught you how to share."

Sighing loudly and rolling her eyes towards the ceiling, she pushed away from the countertop. Straightening her stance, she turned towards him, placing her hands on her hips. Breathing in a breath, then expelling it, she said, "Yes, my mamma did teach me to share, but she isn't here now. I am a grown woman anyhow and I can do what I want, when I want. Furthermore..." she paused and walked right up to him. Looking up at him, she poked a finger in his chest and continued on with her tirade. "It is my chocolate, my hard earned money paid for this, not yours!" After saying the last word, she turned on her three-inch platform sandals and walked away from him.

Resuming her stance at the counter, she went back to her task. Propping her elbows up at the countertop, she once again began to pull five silver foil wrapped chocolate candies from out of the open bag in front of her. Humming along to the Cameo song "Candy" that blasted from a nearby radio, her hips swayed in time to the beat.

He watched as she meticulously unwrapped each individual piece of chocolate and lined them up one by one in a single row. After lining them up in a row, she clasped her hands together, as if in a prayer of thanks. She stood there smiling for a second to admire her handiwork, than uttered one single word, "Perfect!"

A second or two later, her small hands unclasped and she picked up one single chocolate in her right hand. Holding it between two fingers, a pink tongue came out and licked the full lips, and then the chocolate disappeared into the pink mouth. Her dark brown eyes closed as she bit at the candy first, and then sucked at it slowly until it dissolved. The sound that she uttered after eating each piece of chocolate sounded like something that a woman would make after having had good sex. Or at least that was how he would have described it, if someone would have bothered to ask him about it.

This process, this ritual, had been going for about twenty minutes and he had just about enough. She was teasing, torturing him and seemed quite pleased with herself. The air inside of the car garage was humid, hot and so was he. Hotter then a firecracker on the fourth of July, that was what he was. The fan at the end of the countertop didn't even begin to put a damper on the muggy air either. He watched her follow the piece of chocolate with a sip of ice water from a tall glass and cursed loudly. Seething inside, he watched the gauzy skirt of the blue sundress move once again as her hips swayed once more, faster this time. What was the woman thinking anyway, wearing that getup into a car garage? Shit, the little hussy was asking for it, if you asked his opinion! The chocolate was just the icing on the cake. The crowbar that he had been holding in his hand fell to the floor with a loud clang unnoticed as he suddenly stalked towards her.

Upon reaching her, one greased hand grabbed her around the waist and spun her around to face him, while the other reached up to cup her chin. His hips bumped hers up against the countertop, as one hard blue-jean covered leg speared her legs apart. Startled, dark brown eyes widening, her hands came up to rest onto his chest, as a piece of chocolate fell forgotten to the floor.

"What..." was all that she could utter out before his mouth came crashing down on hers. He kissed her then, his tongue stealing inside her parted mouth to taste the chocolate sweetness within. Her hands slid up around his neck, into his hair as her mouth opened wider. He couldn't stop the smile that crossed his lips as he felt the action and his leg pressed harder between her splayed legs. He had just started to stab his tongue deeper inside of her mouth, when all of a sudden she decided to bite him. He let go of her instantly, swearing, his hand flying up to his mouth.

Dark eyes widening in disbelief, he said, "You little she-cat, you bit me!"

Smiling, arms folded across her chest, she said, "Yeah, I suppose that I did. It's not like you didn't deserve it, anyway. Looking down at the grease spots that his hands had left on her blue dress, she said, "This dress is ruined all because of you, these stains will never come out. You are a brute, go away and leave me alone! I should make you buy me another dress, as a matter of fact. Damn you!" The telephone rang just then and, turning back around, she leaned over and picked it up. "Good afternoon, Charles's Garage, Lela speaking. How may I help you?"

He had said nothing during her outraged outburst; instead he had pulled a handkerchief out of his back pocket and wiped it across his bloody bottom lip. After wiping his mouth, he stood still for a second, watching as she talked to the person on the other line. Her face lit up, grinning widely as the person said something of great amusement. Damn, she sure was pretty with her caramel skin, dark brown eyes and full lips, he thought to himself. Okay, he admitted to himself, he had been wrong for ruining that gauzy, sheer thing that she called a dress. But still...his bottom lip hurt like something awful. I really ought to turn over on my knee, he thought as he smiled, imaging the choice words that would come out of that sexy mouth if he were to do so.

She suddenly roared with laughter at something, her elbows once again on the countertop, legs slightly widened, behind stuck out with the phone still pressed tight against her right ear. She is having way too much fun, he thought to himself, still smiling despite the swollen lip. The smile suddenly disappeared as he thought; I wonder who that is on that telephone, one of her many secret admirers? She is such a flirt, tease, and then tries to act so innocent. His eyes fell over her once again and he noticed that her behind stuck out at a very appealing angle. Oh yeah, it was perfect, too easy and before he could help it, laughter escaped from him. She snapped her head around to glare at him sticking her tongue out at him and returned once more to her most oh so interesting conversation.

Eyes gleaming with an unholy light, he once more walked closer to her and knelt down a few feet from her. Pretending to search earnestly for something in the cupboard, he suddenly crawled around to the front of her body. Moving faster then lightening, he reached up under her dress and snatched her pink panties down.

She gasped and almost dropped the phone as soon as she felt her pink panties fall to land on top of her shoes. "What on earth?!" She exclaimed. "No, sorry, it's okay"...she said to the person on the phone. Continuing her conversation with the person on the telephone, she smiled evilly at him and then slapped him hard right across the face.

He smiled up at her outraged expression, choosing to ignore the pain and reached up to cup her bare behind in both of hands. One shoulder held the phone up to her ear as she pushed at his shoulders with both hands in an attempt to get away from him. Her feet entangled by the pink panties however, further hindered her escape though to her displeasure. He had her where he wanted her and decided to take full advantage of the situation too.

Arms holding the backs of her thighs to prevent her from wiggling away, he flipped her dress up. She punched at his shoulders with both hands, the small blows of pain ignored by him as he concentrated on his prize. His knees held her legs immobile as he quickly tied the skirt of the dress up around her waist. The neatly trimmed black nest of curls at the level of his head, he reached around and once more cupped her behind in both hands, pulling her body towards him. Placing a kiss onto the soft flesh just above the curls, he rocked back onto his heels to look up at her.

Smiling into her angry eyes, he said, "Say goodbye and hang up the telephone. Do it now. You might as well give in; I am going to take what I want. I am going to finally get my taste that you denied me. I am not going to go away; I am quite comfortable right here, so stop trying to fight me. Your skin is soft, you smell wonderful and your behind fits perfectly into my hands like it was made for them. I must warn you though; I don't plan on stopping until I make you cum like crazy. I cannot wait to eat you up! So what is your decision?"

She didn't answer him immediately but ceased her fighting, her hands falling to rest lightly on his shoulders. He heard the man's voice on the line inquiring if she was okay when she suddenly went silent. Eyes locked with his, she seemed to have forgotten the person on the other line.

"Well?" he asked. "What is your decision: ya or nay?"

Smiling up at her, he could see her mind working as she debated on what she should do. He knew that he had her though, when she gently smoothed one hand down the side of his face in the same exact spot her slap had landed upon earlier. Her apology, although yet to have been spoken aloud, clearly showed on her face. It grieved her that she had hurt him, that's what he liked about her, her natural caring for others.

She expelled a sigh just then and bid the individual on the telephone goodbye. She then leaned over and dropped the telephone back into its cradle. Returning her attention once more to him she said, "I am so sorry for biting, hurting you. You make me so mad though sometimes, I just fly off at the handle. Please forgive me."

He shook his head at her, saying, "No apology necessary, just bend your knees for me and put your hands onto the countertop. Step out of your panties; Keep the heels on, though. I will help you if you want me to do so; otherwise I will rip them from around your ankles. I want to get my tongue inside you real good. I am so hungry for you, plus your body yearns for it, you want my mouth on you."

"Yes," she said, placing her hands onto the countertop and bending her knees. I have wanted you from the first day that you hired me. I give in, taste me and do unto to me as you wish."

He used his shoulders to widen her thighs open more and then he began to love her with his mouth. Hands and arms braced onto the countertop for support, her hips danced as his lips, tongue, teeth went to work. Eyes closed and gasping for a breathe she struggled to remember to breathe through her mouth, as her whole body shook under his delicious assault. He lowered down further and used his shoulders to make a bigger place for himself between her thighs. His hands squeezed her behind almost painfully as he leaned up into her warmth, his mouth determined to drink the juices that ran out of her. His face mashed up into her wetness as his long tongue licked, sucked, teeth nipped. A couple of seconds later, it was too much, all too much and she started to cum, once then again. Legs shaking, she blanked out and would have fallen to the floor, had he not been holding onto her. He stayed with her the entire time as her wetness dripped out of her into his open mouth.

She came back to herself a few minutes later and opened her wet eyes, to find him placing gentle kisses on her thighs, moist nest of curls and the tops of her thighs. She reached down to clasp his head in both of her hands and their eyes locked for a second. She had just started to say something, when the bell over the door rang out announcing a potential customer or customers. Face flushing; her hands shook as she struggled to untie the knot that he had made in her dress to hold it out of his way. Still on his knees in front of her, his soft hair tickled her stomach as he chuckled, stilling her shaking hands.

"Relax. Relax, stop wiggling," he said. "I got it, stay still. They are going to know that something is going on, with the way that you are acting. You are acting like a kid who just caught with their hand in the cookie jar. I don't have time to move away, but just stay still and I will do likewise. I am going to untie this and let your dress cover up my head, okay. The countertop is high enough for nobody to see a thing, so don't worry about it."

The dress had just fallen down to cover his head when a man walked up to the counter. Looking at her with touch of concern, he said, "I know that it is hot out and forgive me for being so forward, but miss you don't look so well. You are perspiring and your face is quite flushed. Are you okay?"

Licking her lips, she brought a hand up to brush back a lock of her sweaty dark brown hair and said, "It's just this heat. I am afraid that the piece of junk fan doesn't put out that much air and the air conditioner isn't working. My boss has neglected to get it fixed as of yet." She let out a small gasp suddenly when her right thigh was subjected to a pinch at the mention of the air conditioner.

Pasting a fake smile on her face when the man gave her a strange look, her left hand slipped down under the counter to twist at an ear through the fabric of her dress. She was rewarded with a soft bite onto the soft flesh just about her curls. Struggling to focus on the man standing in front of her, she silently pleaded for the sexy devil between her legs to behave.

"Sir, I am fine, thanks so much for your concern though. How may I assist you?"

"I need twenty-five dollars worth of gas on pump five," the man said, still eyeing her strangely. He handed her a twenty and a five and then said, "I hope for your sake that the boss gets the air fixed soon, otherwise he may have a sick employee on his hands soon enough. You have a good day now."

As soon as the door closed behind the man, the sexy devil crawled out from between her legs and stood up to his full six foot, one inch height. Looking down at her as he shoved her pink panties into his back pocket, he said, "Flushed, eh? Sweetheart, the man was just too polite to say the obvious. Your nipples are so hard, they are flushed right up against that thin piece of lace you call a bra." He turned away then, laughing at the look of horror that came onto her face. Priceless, he thought to himself, absolutely priceless.

# The Visitor

He came to visit me one hot summer night

Knelt down beside my bed and whispered to me that everything would be all right

Between my black silk sheets he did glide

My eyes went wide with fright as he slowly begin to spread my feet

Legs of the heaviest muscle forcefully pushed against mine

And it was then that I realized his intent and I braced myself, preparing to live, to fight

Granted he was far stronger than I, but determination gave me a will to try

Me, being of a petite statue, was no match for his steely embrace; he smiled at my efforts as he gently cupped my face

The butterfly kiss he bestowed upon my lips, reassured me that he was true to his word and indeed did not mean me any harm

Sweetest nectar, I had ever tasted was left upon my tongue, so rich and smooth, almost like a well aged rum

Ecstasy shot through my body as it flew through time and space

Last, night, last, dawn I silently prayed, please do not come so fast

Night, I fear though crept away and as the sun started to arise, he arose and vanished right before my sleep deprived eyes

Read the first word of each sentence and in them you will find a fantasy statement

### The Naughty Professor I

They had been chatting for a few minutes when he suddenly stopped talking and just looked at her for a second. Then he said, "Turn around." Picking up a small paperback book from a nearby bookcase, he said, "You need a spanking, you need to be spanked."

"Really?" she asked, smiling at him, her interest piqued, "Do you really think so? I have been spanked before. Well, okay if you insist." She turned around and stuck out her brown corduroy covered bottom.

A few seconds later he brought the book down and it connected with her bottom. He didn't hit her hard, but it was with just enough aggression to let her know that he was the ruler in the bedroom.

The butt spanking made her want him even more, she realized as she took a nearby seat, her gaze fixed upon him. Green eyes stared into her dark brown ones as he licked his lips. Without looking down to confirm it to be true, she felt her pointed nipples press harder against the cotton fabric of her bra.

Still looking at her, he walked to a nearby table, placed both hands palm flat down on top of it, stuck out his butt and spread his legs slightly. Feet flat on the floor, he used his forearms to hold his body upright as he turned towards her and said, "What you need to do is get yourself some. That's your problem, go and stand in front of a man like this. No man can resist a stance like this, believe me."

Gazing at him, eyes wide, she said, "I am a good girl, though. I usually wait for the man to make the first move. I don't do things like that, that's just not me."

Standing up straight, he went back to stacking some papers into a pile, his back to her as he said, "I know you are a good girl, I never said that you weren't. Men don't respect women they just met who give it up, anyway. I mean, I am not saying that I haven't done that before, but that's not the point. If you were not a good girl, we probably would have already done something by now, completely forgetting about everybody and everything. I understand, though, that you need cock and there is nothing wrong with that either."

She listened to all of this, her dark brown eyes thoughtful, not saying anything. He was right of course; she did enjoy cock and it had been awhile for her, about six months or so. At this point though, she really wanted to be kissed and boy did look quite kissable. "Hmm," ...she thought. The next time that he asked for some chap stick, she just might offer him some; from her lips to his, that is. Or perhaps the next time she hugged him from the back, she just might let her hand accidentally slip down and.... She suddenly smiled wide with utter delight. He was going to get it, oh yes he was!

The very next day she saw him, but things time were different. They had audience for one, but he still insisted on coming up close beside her to say in a low voice, "You need a spanking. Yes, you do."

She chose to ignore his devilish statement, but inside she secretly plotted to make him pay for it later on.

## The Naughty Professor II

Coming up behind him, she placed her arms around his shoulders, hands upon his chest. She hugged his head to her generous chest for a minute, and then leaned down to whisper into his left ear, "What would you do if I told you that I just went into the bathroom and removed my panties?"

Calmly removing her arms from around his shoulders, and without uttering a single word, he slowly turned around in his chair. Stepping back from him, she watched as he stood to his feet and carefully placed the textbook that he had been reading onto his chair. Then he walked towards her, so very close, until they stood nose to nose. He seductively held her dark brown gaze with his green one the entire time. She had stopped breathing by then; her mouth parted slightly, her heart beating fast as she waited to see what he would do.

Licking his lips slowly, he moved back a couple of steps from her and said, "Get your ass up on that desk, right now!"

Trembling slightly, she walked past him and, pushing a couple of books aside, she made herself a place to sit on the desk.

He walked towards her then, stopping about four feet from her and said, "Spread your legs wide and pull up that skirt for me." Holding his gaze with hers, she did as he asked. Spreading her legs and tugging up her skirt, she struggled to breathe, her tongue flickering out to lick her suddenly dry lips.

He walked between her spread legs and calmly reached down to unzip the fly of his slacks. They stared into each other's eyes as, with one hand, he pushed her skirt higher. With his other hand he pulled his cock from out of his boxers.

She had one brief second to look down and notice that his hard, swollen cock had been covered with a condom before he pushed into her hard. Her startled gasp was quickly swallowed up by his mouth covering hers. Her hands came up to gasp his forearms, his shoulders, as her legs wrapped around his waist. The black sandals that had been on her pink toes fell to the floor, unnoticed.

He leaned over her, and she fell back onto the desk as his hips begin to move. His hips moved to a dance of their own making, cock driving deep into her aching vaginal walls. One of his hands braced her body against the desk, while his other hand wrapped themselves into her dark brown strands to fuse their mouths together. Their lips drank from each others, as tongues slid across one another. All the while, a hard, swollen cock squeezed itself inside of her small, drenched opening.

He pulled away from her mouth to whisper in her ear, "I surprised you, didn't I? You didn't expect me to be waiting, willing, protected and ready to go, did you? This is what you wanted isn't it? All of those damn teasing notes, sneaky little hugs, making sure that I felt your boobs against me! You wanted me to lose control and you succeeded. Proud of yourself, huh? You wanted my cock in between your caramel thighs; you hungered for it, didn't you?"

The last statement that came from his lips was just enough to send her over the edge. Shoving her hands deep into his dark-brown hair, she kissed him letting him swallow her cry of release with his mouth. A second later, he began to cum. Even through the condom she could feel his warm sperm. The feel of his essence trigged another climax from her, causing her muscles to clamp down harder around his cock, milking him. He pulled out of her a few seconds later and removed the condom. Pulling a tissue from a nearby box, he wiped his cock clean and zipped his slacks back up.

Shocked beyond belief that they had 'done the deed' on a desk, out in the opening where anyone at anytime could have walked in, she hurriedly pushed her skirt back down around her hips.

He turned to walk out of the classroom, but not before saying, "I believe that you have just earned yourself an 'A'. Now you better get out of here before someone walks in. You also just might want to make another trip to the bathroom, as well. Your face is quite flushed and you smell like sex; a woman who has had good sex, I might add."

He laughed aloud then turned and walked out the door.

## *The Rules*

"Some rules are not meant to be broken," she said holding his gaze, backing away from him.

Smiling at her, he continued advancing closer and closer towards her.

Hands clasped behind her back, she suddenly found herself up against the wall. Bumping his hips against hers, he reached up and cupped her face with both hands. Her palms flat against the wall behind her, her dark brown eyes began to widen as she stared into his dancing green eyes. Mouth slightly parted, she struggled to remember to breathe.

Tilting her head to the side, he placed his lips close to her left ear and whispered, "Funny… you were not thinking about any rules the other night. Correct me if I am wrong, but I distinctively remember your caramel thighs locked tightly around my head."

She let out a moan, her eyes drifting closed. Her hands came up to bury themselves into his blondish-brown wavy hair. Her mouth was watering as she was desperate for his kiss.

He resisted her, licking the shell of her ear first. Then he whispered, "Is that what you want? My mouth covering your vanilla scented lips? My tongue licking inside to taste your wet warmth?"

## *A Forbidden Passion*

Looking around her nervously, she unconsciously chewed on her bottom lip. Could they tell that she was naïve? Twenty-eight and she had never once sinned. The woman across from her gave her a half-smile and then went back to the newspaper in front of her. The man next to her had his nose buried in a Popular Mechanics magazine and ignored her completely.

Just then, the motors roared to life and the plane started to move down the runway. Facing straight-ahead, she held her breath slightly; she had never been that good at flying, for some reason.

"Breathe, breathe," she silently chanted to herself, "Breathe and nothing bad will happen."

Taking a deep, ragged breath, she let her mind drift back to the night before. Most people read a novel before falling asleep; she had read the brochure for the twentieth time. The embarrassing (and oh, so very naughty) brochure that had gone into the greatest detail about all the delights it offered to satisfy one's needs. Delicious and decadent, it made her think of smooth, creamy milk chocolate every time she read it.

But it was the toy that she had remembered the most about last night. She felt her face heat slightly as she recalled how wonderful it had made her feel. The resort had enclosed a sample, so to speak, of what pleasures the guest could expect. Enclosed inside of a tiny, discreet, brown package had been a tongue tickler. Pink in coloring, the toy was soft and flexible on one side, and had tiny ridges on the other side. A small sheet of paper with instructions printed on it had been included in the package, as well.

Irene had stared at the contraption in general confusion at first. Turning the object over and over in her hands, she had searched in vain for any clue to what its purpose might be. Curiosity had gotten the best of her a second later and, placing the object down on her nightstand, she had picked up the set of instructions. As she began to read, involuntarily her mouth dropped opened in shocked fascination.

A few moments later, she had picked the tickler up, found the 'on' button, and switched the setting onto 'low'. Then, raising her hips she reached under her short Victoria's Secrets nightshirt, removed her pink cotton panties. She had lain back down and let her thighs fall open as she very carefully placed the tickler between the lips of her vagina.

Her breath sucked in as she felt the first gentle touch of the tickler; her thighs closed around it and that is when the sensations really began to kick in. The tickler slid forward, then backward, reaching deep into her virginal vagina walls. She had groaned and closed her legs tighter around the tickler, with the smooth part of the tickler forward and the ridged side backward. The sensations were incredible; smooth, then slightly rough.

Soon the nightshirt became too hot, too suffocating. Licking her lips, she sat up and pulled it over her head, throwing it across the room. She then laid back down, but not before turning the tickler to the medium setting. The tickler soon became slippery wet with her juices. Her clit became swollen as she wallowed in ecstasy. She cupped her breasts in both hands, pulling at the pointed nipples, moaning, her hips lifting. She had never experienced such pleasure in her life.

It had been only a few minutes later, that she had her first orgasm in twenty-eight years. Irene, naked, sweaty and dripping wet from her orgasm, had snuggled down into her satin blue sheets and had fallen fast asleep with a smile on her face.

Coming back to reality, she sighed and twirled a strand of dark brown hair around her index finger, thinking. Her mother would literally fall down on her knees in prayer crying, "Baby girl, why would you want to do something like that? It is just the devil working!"

Her mother was a mess; she had already flipped out

when she had found out that Irene had gone on the pill.

Irene's doctor had put her on the pill in order to control

her menstrual cycle.

Irene's friends would say that she was flat out

crazy. She had made up her mind though; it was time

for this release, screw it. Confidentiality and privacy

were two of the main reasons why she had chosen the

resort in the first place. The passion had been buried

inside of her too damn long.

She snapped out of her musings a few minutes

later when the flight attendant asked if she wanted

lunch or not. She was starving, having only drunk a

glass of orange juice that morning and it was now noon.

However, she seriously doubted that anything would

stay put; her stomach was indeed tied up in knots. So,

despite her hunger, she asked only for a diet Sprite to

drink instead.

The flight was an hour and a half and she figured that it would take about forty minutes or so to make it through customs. The brochure stated that a chauffeured car would be waiting at the airport for her. She started to silently pray that nothing would go wrong, and then she stopped herself. She seriously doubted that any Gods would approve of what she was about to do.

An hour and a half later, the plane landed on the runway. She waited impatiently for the seatbelt sign to go off and then stood up to gather her carry-on bag. The man next to her stood as well and quickly gathered his carry-on bag, too. When he stood, she got a glimpse of his clean-shaven square jaw, long nose, and full lips. She couldn't help thinking, "Wow! He is hot, with his bald head and toffee colored skin."

He stood around six feet, three inches or so, being roughly about the same height as her friend Jon.

Ignoring her, he brushed against her in his hurry to leave the plane.

"Rude," she thought as she followed the lean, broad shouldered figure in front of her. "An arrogant ass, he is probably used to women ogling him." The scent of his cologne teased her nose and the woman in her jumped to awareness. "Damn him," she thought to herself as she continued through customs.

She grabbed her suitcase off the spinning carousel and, straightening her shoulders, walked on. "He paid no attention to you of course; it is not as if that has never happened before." The tiny voice of reasoning seemed to mock her, making her fragile self-esteem go down a notch. "Maybe this was a mistake," she thought to herself, as she handed her passport to the customs officer. However, she thought about how much money that she had spent for this week-long trip and determinedly walked on through the exit doors.

Glancing around for any sign of the chauffeured car, her gaze once again landed on the man from the plane. Leaning against one of the columns of the building, he spoke rapidly into the cell phone that was glued to his ear. Dark aviator sunglasses covered the eyes that she never had the chance to see the color of. Sighing, she turned away and continued to search for the driver.

Just then, a long black limousine pulled up to the curb. The driver's door opened and a medium-height, suntanned young man wearing dark sunglasses hopped out. Blond haired, he was casually dressed in a short-sleeved buttoned-down shirt, black knee-length shorts and flip-flops. Stepping up onto the sidewalk with a smile, he stopped in front of her and said, "Ms. Irene Cooper?"

"This is it," she thought, "There is no going back now."

She licked her suddenly dry lips and said, "Yes, that's me." She wondered how the man knew who she was, until she realized what she had on. The tiny silver dolphin pinned on the left side of her chest clearly identified her to the driver.

He smiled at her response and said, "My name is Andrew. Welcome to Puerto Rico."

"Thank you," she said, with a half a smile of her own.

Opening the back door for her, he said, "Ms. Cooper, please get in and help yourself to any refreshment of your choice from the mini bar. There are further instructions for you to read in the folder on the seat as well. I will take care of your bags for you. Make yourself comfortable."

Once seated, she looked around and thought, "Wow! This is the life!" The mini bar was stocked with several bottles of ice water, soft drinks and liqueur of every kind. A bottle of expensive champagne sat chilling in a nearby ice chest. In a glass case on one shelf there was a platter of assorted cheeses, crackers, and fruit. However, what really caught her attention was the sizeable television with an attached DVD player hanging from the ceiling of the limo. She decided on a bottle of water and picked up the folder beside her to read.

Quickly reading the basic welcome information, she continued on to the instructions listed beneath 'First Day, Number 1': "In order to fully free themselves to the full extent, clients must remove all underwear before entering into the compound. Female clients will have the choice to remove bra or panties/thong, etc, but not both. The male chauffer/driver will remove the garment that the female has not removed herself.

The same rule applies to the male client. The male client will have the choice to remove either his shirt or his underwear. The female chauffer/ driver will remove the garment that he has not removed himself.

Failure to comply with either or all of these instructions will result in instant disqualification of the program. After breaking the contract and signing a privacy statement, a partial refund would be refunded to the individual in question within thirty days.

Transportation to the airport would be provided for the client at no extra charge. However, the client will be on his or her own concerning the cost of a return flight. If you have any questions, please refer to the rules and regulations in the brochure that you should have received in the mail prior to registering.

Please press the play button on the DVD player if you understand and agree with the instructions printed here."

She swallowed, her eyes widening as she though over the agreement for a minute.

"Oh my goodness, what have I got myself into?" she asked herself. Then, shrugging her shoulders, she sighed. "What the hell; this is what I wanted right?"

Leaning over, she pressed the play button on the DVD player in front of her. Andrew's face appeared on the screen and he began to tell her what to expect of the week ahead. The compound was located near the water, so many of the activities involved the water as a result. There were daily spa treatments, sport activities, nature walks, etc. They included the usual activities that you would expect from a vacation, except for the daily list of naughty activities each day. Clients would not know what the naughty activity was until that morning the event was to take place.

The DVD also showed the property and grounds of the compound, giving a brief tour of the facilities. Locked behind huge gates, it was surrounded by lush greenery and trees, ensuring complete privacy. "A paradise of tempting treats in an exotic country just waiting to be explored," she thought, admiring the beautiful sights in front of her. Five minutes later, the screen went blue as the DVD ended.

The partition between the driver and the back seat slid down. Andrew, his eyes shaded from the sun in sunglasses, smiled at her in the rearview mirror. "Ms. Cooper," he said, "From now on, we will be on a first name basis for the duration of the trip. Of course, if you would prefer, you can also use a nickname if it would make you more comfortable. However, I assure you that our resort is well known for its confidentiality. We will be arriving at the compound in about ten more minutes. I suggest that you decide which garment that you would like to remove and do so now. I will put something easy and soft in the CD player to get you in the mood."

As soon as he finished speaking, he removed his sunglasses and winked at her with dancing, vivid-blue eyes. Still smiling, he slid the partition closed once again and soft music began to emit from the speakers in the ceiling.

She debated for a few minutes, bra or panties. Panties, she decided after a minute, as she was not ready for a strange man to get between her legs just yet. Every time that she went to the GYN doctor for her yearly, she dreaded it. Then she thought with a shrug, "Stop being a prude, this is what you wanted right? No inhibitions, freedom to do what you pleased just because it felt right at the time."

After finishing that thought, she found herself slowly pulling up her short denim skirt. Sliding her hands up under the skirt and wiggling her hips slightly, she removed her powder blue panties underneath. She supposed that the statement concerning the removal of her underwear should not have surprised her. The brochure had suggested that underwear of any kind would be optional. However, the brochure had clearly stated that top clothes were required due to health concerns. Although a place to free and satisfy client's needs, it did not encourage complete nudity.

Her hands were slightly clammy as she carefully folded her panties and placed them into the clear plastic bag that had been provided for them. She was nervous, wondering what he would think about her breasts. She had once been overweight and had just recently lost some of the weight. Consequently, she did have some sagging in her breasts, despite the weight lifting that she had been doing for the last few months.

All too soon, the car rolled to a stop and she heard the driver's door open. A minute later, Andrew opened the back door and got in and sat on the seat across from her. Grinning mischievously at her, he asked, "Which article of clothing do I get the pleasure of removing?"

Licking her lips, she said in a small voice, "My bra."

"Delighted," he said. "Kindly remove your shirt."

Taking a deep breath, she did as he asked and placed it on the seat beside her.

"Nice," he said with a wink. "I do admire full breasted women." Her face was slightly heated, but inside she was secretly pleased. He told her to turn around and get on her knees between his spread legs, so that her back was to him. She did as he asked, feeling the cool, soft rug on her recently shaved legs.

Smoothing his hands across her shoulders and cupping her neck, he urged her chin up. Then, leaning down to her ear, he whispered, "Look up above the seat where you are sitting."

She did and let out a slight gasp, a long panel mirror ran the length of the seat. She could clearly see her and Andrew's reflections in it. He leaned back, smoothing his hands down her back, and stopped at the catch of her powder blue bra. "Don't take your eyes off of the mirror, watch my hands," he said. Trembling

slightly, she did as he asked. His huge hands felt

slightly rough against her soft back. "Feel," he

whispered and then his fingers snapped the clasp of her

bra.

The cloth moved aside, eager to display its bounty

and involuntarily her hands shot up to cover her

breasts. Letting out a laugh, he said, "Uh-uh, no way.

Let go." Biting her lips, her eyes pleaded with his in the

mirror, but he shook his head 'No' at her silent request.

"It's the only way; Relax, feel and look. You can do

whatever you want: swear, moan, anything."

She removed her hands and huge warm palms

quickly replaced hers. She shivered at his touch-

strange, yet, oh so exciting.

"You know," he said, musing aloud, "I have

always liked satin on a woman. It just molds to her

skin." As he talked, his hands began to massage her

breasts through the thin material. Around and around

his hand moved, agonizingly slow, as she struggled to breathe. With her eyes glued to the mirror, the sensations were incredible and her breasts seemed to grow bigger with each pass of his hands. Her nipples started to ache and became erect, begging for attention as well. The satin, combined with the movements of his hands, made her nipples stand out like overripe cherries.

"I wonder if I can make you cum just from playing with your tits?" he pondered, winking at her in the mirror.

Moaning, she breathed out a single word, "Please."

He grinned widely and suddenly let the bra fall to the floor. She felt just one small brush of air before his hands once more returned to their bounty. He moved his hands in smaller circles on her tits, just missing her yearning pointed nipples. "What do you need, Irene? Tell me," he encouraged softly in her ear.

Moaning, back arching, knees slightly trembling, she gasped, "Touch me, please."

"Where?" he breathed back in her ear.

"My nipples, damn you!" she gasped, her fingernails slightly digging into his knees.

He laughed, delighted with her response, and then said, "Okay, just one more thing." Removing one hand from her breasts, he reached over, opened the mini fridge and grabbed an ice-cold bottle of water. "Open your legs a little wider and pull up your skirt."

"Wha...what are you doing?" she asked, surfacing out of her sensual fog.

"Trust me," he said. She paused for a second, and then did as he asked. He shoved the bottle between her legs. The cold, wet bottle shocked her speechless as first and she started to speak, "Andrew, I...."

He grinned and said, "I know what you need. Now close your legs around the bottle and feel."

She did as he asked and felt the hard, cold bottle resting against her own wetness. The bottle had just the right amount of hardness to annoy the super-sensitized little nub of flesh between her furry thatch. It felt wonderful, she admitted to herself, but Andrew was not finished with her. He went back to playing with her tits, his fingers lightly pinching her swollen nipples, repeatedly.

"Come on," he said in her ear. "Squeeze your legs together harder, feel it." She was almost there, she felt it. Her thighs grasped the bottle tighter, her back arched, as she struggled to breathe. Then suddenly he reached over, grabbed the bottle by its cap and turned it counter clockwise once; it was just enough. She came then, hard, her whole body shaking, her shout of release filling the car. She sat down abruptly. The bottle fell from between her slack thighs as she struggled to breathe. Smacking a kiss on her forehead, he picked her up and laid her on the seat. He opened the door to get out, then turned around and picked the still wet

bottle of water up. She lay there, seemingly unaware of

her nakedness; her body drained but satisfied, her skirt

still up around her hips. With her legs slightly spread,

she was no longer shy. Her heavy breasts, nipples

slightly distended, were pillowed on her chest.

Opening the bottle of water, he paused before

drinking to say, "Welcome to Paradise Island.  Damn,

but you are easy! Get dressed, we will be at the resort

in a few minutes," and winking he took a sip of water.

Reaching back inside the limo, he picked up her bra

from the floor, along with the plastic bag containing her

underwear, and shut the door. She laid still, her body

numb, for a few minutes before she sat up and pulled

her shirt on and slid the skirt back down over her hips.

A few minutes later, the car pulled up to a tall

gate that swung open after Andrew had rolled down the

window and pressed a button on the side mirror. Irene

fell in love with the lush greenery that grew in

abundance as they drove into the resort. Exotic flowers colored the grounds around the buildings. The waterfall in the center of the circular driveway was huge. A statue of the Greek goddess Aphrodite stood over the fountain. Andrew stopped in front of a pale peach building with cream-colored doors. He got out, came around to the back of the limo and opened the door for her.

As she stepped out of the car, the cream-colored doors of the building opened and a petite, dark haired woman stepped out. Wearing a sheer pink blouse, white capris, and black high-heeled sandals on her feet, the woman walked towards them.

"Hello," she said, addressing Irene. "Welcome to Paradise Island." She held out an arm to Irene and they shook hands. "My name is Angelique. I will be your personal assistant for the duration of your stay. Andrew," she said, turning towards him. "How was the trip?"

Andrew, with Irene's bags in tow, said, "We had a nice time." He winked at both of them, handing the plastic bag with Irene's underwear in it to Angelique.

Angelique laughed and said, "Good." Irene felt her face heat, but she ignored the sensation and refused to be embarrassed. Angelique took the bag and, turning back to Andrew, asked him to take Irene's bags to her room on the seventh floor. Turning back to Irene, she said, "The view is incredible and you will get to see some marvelous sunsets while you are here. Please follow me."

The two of them walked through the cream-colored doors into the main hotel. The lobby of the hotel was spacious and decorated with potted plants everywhere. The high ceilings, painted white, had huge fans that kept a steady breeze blowing throughout the lobby. Several people were seated on the dark chocolate wicker couches spread all around. In the middle of the lobby was a water fountain with the marble figures of a man and a woman intertwined in a passionate embrace. Water sluiced over the two lovers frozen in time.

Angelique walked to the front desk, handed the plastic bag with Irene's underwear in it to the woman behind the counter and said, "Irene Cooper, checking in."

The young woman, who looked around sixteen, smiled at the two of them. Irene knew that she had to be at least twenty-one though, because the resort was for adults only. Angelique said, "This is Tara. She works the front desk and helps out anywhere else if needed."

"Welcome Irene," Tara said. "I hope that you enjoy your stay with us and please do not hesitate to call if you need anything. Dialing 08 on your telephone can reach the front desk directly. You can pick up this at checkout time, okay?" Tara indicated the bag that contained Irene's underwear before she placed a sticker on the outside of it.

"Thanks, Tara," Angelique said. "Please, follow me, Irene. Are you hungry? I will show you to the dining room. Afterwards, I will take you on a tour of the facility, okay?" Irene conceded that she was indeed hungry and followed Angelique to the dining room.

Later that night, after taking a leisure bath in a bathtub big enough for two or more people, Irene fell asleep with a smile on her face. Feeling deliciously wicked, she slept nude for the first time in her life on gold satin sheets.

********

The next morning, at around eight in the morning, she awoke to the door of her suite opening up. Angelique came in bearing a breakfast tray with a smile on her pretty face.

"Wake up sleepyhead," she said grinning. "You have a big day ahead of you. I hope that you are up to the challenge."

Irene sat up, holding the top sheet to her chest. "Morning Angelique," she said sleepily. "Hmm, something smells wonderful."

Angelique placed the tray on the stand beside the bed, then walked over to the curtains and spread them open. Turning back around to face Irene, she said, "It is going to be a beautiful day. Eat up and I will be back to see you in about another forty-five minutes or so. Is that enough time for you to get dressed?"

Irene paused in the act of spreading strawberry cream cheese on her blueberry bagel and said, "Sure, that's fine. Thanks, Angelique, for everything."

A few minutes later the door shut behind Angelique and Irene commenced to enjoy the warm bagel and the egg white omelet filled with cheese, chives, mushrooms and jalapeño peppers. The orange juice, freshly squeezed, and the cantaloupes were the perfect accompanist to the cold Starbucks coffee. After eating, Irene hopped into the shower. A few minutes later, she pulled on a matching peach bra and panty set and a short-sleeved sundress. In front of the mirror, she applied light foundation, black eyeliner and a plum lipstick to complete her make-up. As she began to brush the shoulder-length brown hair, she wondered what the days' naughty agenda included. She was just slipping her feet into a pair of high-heeled sandals, when Angelique knocked on the door and walked in.

"Here is your list of today's events," Angelique said with a twinkle in her eyes, handing Irene a medium-sized blue envelope.

"Thanks, Angelique," she said and carefully slit open the sealed envelope with the silver letter opener that she had found on the dresser. She read the enclosed blue card with utter delight!--"Day 2- Nymphs, nymphs everywhere! Today you will experience a spa treatment exclusively for you, which cannot be found anywhere!"

"A spa treatment, how wonderful!" she exclaimed.

Angelique said, "You are going to love it. Follow me, please."

As Irene followed Angelique through the beautiful hotel, she could not help glancing curiously at the people around her. She sucked in a breath when her eyes collided with a pair of gorgeous green eyes. It was him- the man from the plane; she finally had the chance to see his eyes and it had been well worth the wait. He held her gaze for a minute, then winked at her and turned back to the conversation that he had been having with a dark-brown haired man and a blond haired woman. Irene, embarrassed to have been caught staring, turned and hurried after Angelique.

Having seen who Stephen had winked at, looking after Irene, Robert asked, "Who was that?"

Stephen took a sip of the beer in his hand, and then said, "Oh, just a woman from the plane who got caught staring. She has nice eyes, but that is about it."

Looking slightly amused, Robert said, "Oh really? She seems to have liked what she saw, as she was able to recognize you automatically. You know what I am; a leg man. She does have a nice pair."

Stephen laughed and said, "You are crazy man, but hey- it's whatever rocks your boat."

Irene, blissfully unaware of their comments, walked into a pale blue room behind Angelique. Thick matching carpet covered the floor. Native American flute music floated out from the invisible speakers. Low lights and a long table, adorned with caramel-colored cushions, dominated the room. A white satin sheet and a pillow rested on the table. A small aquarium, filled with brightly colored fish, took up one wall of the room. Next to the main table sat a smaller table with several fluffy, white towels and various hair-brushes, and glass bottles of oils and lotions.

Angelique saw Irene's awed expression and said, "The object of this room is for the client to experience total and complete relaxation. First, Irene, even though you look nice, I am going to ask that you remove your clothing." Pointing to a closed door on one side of the room, she said, "You can change in that room. There is also a shower, towels and robes in there for your convenience. I will be out here waiting, take as long as you need to."

Irene walked through the door that Angelique had indicated to and began to undress. Removing her bra and panties, she decided to take another shower for good measure. She had just stepped into the shower when the curtain was drawn back. Gasping, she took a step back and attempted to cover her private parts.

Angelique stood before her in a black bikini and smiled at her. "It's okay, it's just little ole me. I thought that you might need some help."

Irene started to say, "I don't think ..."

Angelique said once again, "It is okay; we both have the same anatomy, relax. Now do you want for me to help you wash your hair?"

Irene swallowed and said, "Yes, please."

Angelique, looking amused, said, "You are shy still, but by the time that I am done with you, your shyness will have disappeared. Turn around so that your back is to me."

Irene did as she was told and Angelique stepped in behind her. Irene closed her eyes and waited. A few seconds later, Angelique began to message apple scented shampoo into Irene's hair. Angelique's nimble fingers carefully spread the shampoo throughout her strands. She could not help letting a moan of satisfaction escape from between her lips. Angelique massaged her hair a few minutes then said, "Lean back a little bit more for me, so that I can rinse it out. You don't need any conditioner; the shampoo has conditioner included already."

Angelique stepped out of the shower and, removing her bikini, dried off with a fluffy white towel. Slipping on a white satin robe, she held out a towel for Irene to step into. Irene stepped out and toweled off, then slipped on a satin white robe of her own. She placed a dry towel around her wet hair.

When the two of them walked back into the massage room, Tara, dressed in an identical robe, was waiting for them. Angelique smiled and said, "She is almost ready." Turning to Irene she said, "Please remove your robe and towel and lie face down on the table. There is a step stool to use if you need it."

Irene did as she was told, sliding onto her stomach and placing her head on her folded arms. She closed her eyes and waited. The soft, smooth sheet felt incredibly cool against her skin. She felt a little embarrassed at first by her bottom being on display, then thought, "We are all women here, so it is okay." Moments later, a calming saxophone melody began to emit from the walls of the room. The delicious aroma of coconut filled the room as Angelique said, "Tara and I will work together to make you relax, okay? Trust us."

A hairdryer came on and Angelique's nimble fingers began to comb through Irene's hair, drying the wet locks. Tara, in the main time, had begun to smooth the warm coconut oil across Irene's back. About ten minutes later, when Angelique finished her first task, she joined Tara in smoothing the oil over Irene's body.

Irene let out a sigh and relaxed, her body warming slightly. Eyes closed, she concentrated on the wailing sax and the delicious smell of the oil. Her eyes popped opened when she felt Angelique's hands daringly brush the sides of her breasts. Angelique met her startled eyes with a smile and said, "Relax. Just feel and trust me. Close your eyes again, okay?"

Irene tentatively did as she was told, but after a few minutes her eyes popped opened again when she felt Tara's hands spreading the cheeks of her ass to smooth oil in between the crease.

Angelique cooed in her, "It is okay, trust me."

Trembling slightly, Irene rested her head back down on her folded arms and closed her eyes once again. Angelique's hands swept across her shoulders, back and spine a few more times then returned to the sides of her breasts. Tara messaged each cheek of her bottom several times and then returned to the crease in between. One long, slender finger drew oil down the crease from top to bottom. A little nervous, but excited, Irene started to feel herself lifting her chest slightly so that Angelique could have better access to her tits. Her legs spread to give Tara better access to her behind. Her body felt feverish and she found herself having to bite back a moan. Suddenly the hands stopped moving over her body and her eyes popped opened.

Angelique said, "Please turn over, so that we can finish."

Embarrassed, Irene did as she was asked. It had been okay to feel excited, hell, aroused when her eyes had been closed, lost in her own private world; But when her eyes were open, things were different. Face slightly red, she silently cursed her swollen, pointed, nipples and the gathering wetness between her legs. Pressing her legs together, she closed her eyes once again.

Angelique said, "You can open your eyes. You don't have to feel embarrassed or ashamed, your response to our ministrations is perfectly normal. Tara and I enjoyed it as much as you did."

Irene opened her eyes and turned her head to look at Angelique. She let out a gasp when she saw that

Angelique was naked. Angelique's body was beautiful; there were no other words to describe it. Short, black curls framed a pixie looking face, with full red lips. Her olive complexion was the perfect canvas for her figure, slightly full tits with swollen chocolate brown nipples and a flat stomach. A neatly trimmed nest of tightly black curls rested between short, but slender legs.

Angelique said, "Now look to your left, towards Tara."

Irene did and saw that she was also naked. Her straight brown hair was slung over one shoulder, her high, firm breasts on full display. She had pink, pointed nipples resting on swollen flesh, a slightly round tummy and a mop of neatly trimmed brown curls between her long legs. Irene should have been embarrassed, horrified, to even gaze upon their naked flesh, yet she did not feel any of those things. Instead, she felt amazed, aroused and wondered.

"Does this make me a lesbian? Or on the other hand, am I just sexually uninhibited and appreciative of beautiful female bodies?" she wondered to herself.

A second later, she shocked herself when she said, "Angelique, Tara I trust the two of you. Do whatever you want to me; I want it all."

Angelique gave her a wide grin, then said, "Relax and feel free to do whatever you want to Tara and myself as well. Close your eyes if you want to, or leave them open."

Angelique moved to stand behind Irene and Tara moved to stand at her feet. Irene thought about closing her eyes, but found that she could not do so. Angelique began to rub her shoulders, than she slid her oily hands to Irene's full breasts to massage oil onto them, as well. Since Angelique was leaning over Irene's head to massage her breasts, Irene had an excellent view of her tits; they hung directly above her face, swinging slightly, just begging to be kissed. Irene debated what to do for a second and then leaned her head up to take a lick of one nipple. The taste was incredible. The soft, pointy tip glistened and Irene found herself wanting to do more. Angelique had moaned at the first touch of her tongue. Her hands that had been shaping Irene's tits now started to rub and pull at Irene's distended nipples.

"Do what you want," Angelique said.

Irene had been so busy concentrating on Angelique's breasts that she had almost forgotten about Tara. Tara, who had been rubbing her thighs, now had spread them open. Irene opened her legs wider to give her a full view.

Tara said, "Don't be alarmed, but I am going to trim you just a little, okay?" She pulled out a pair of scissors and proceeded to clip the stray hairs that surrounded Irene's bush. The cold scissors teased at Irene's swollen flesh before they were replaced with Tara's fingers.

Beyond caring how brazen she had become, Irene moaned and arched her head so that her mouth could once again latch onto Angelique's nipple. Nipping it between her teeth, she loved the sound that Angelique made, and decided to suckle the soft flesh. Angelique pinched Irene's nipples in response to the tugging and biting of Irene's mouth. Meanwhile, Tara, having finished trimming Irene's curls, lowered her head and began to lick between Irene's legs. Her fingers opened the curls and sought out the hidden nub of flesh, while her tongue lapped at the wetness. Finding what she had sought, Tara began to bite and suckle the highly sensitive bud between her lips.

Irene was in pure ecstasy: two gorgeous women were pleasing her. Angelique played with her nipples while Tara ate between her legs. Moaning, she spread her legs wider and shoved one hand on Tara's head to hold her in place, determined to feel every bite, every lick. Arching up off the table, she latched onto

Angelique's tit and sucked harder, while her other hand pulled at the nipple of its twin. Angelique swore and leaned over further so that her breasts were easier to reach. Her fingers painfully pinched at Irene's nipples but Irene did not care. The sensations became too much all too soon and suddenly Irene screamed. She came once, then twice, her orgasm making her body bow. Angelique's nipple fell out of her mouth and she let go of Tara's hair.

"Wow!" Irene said a few minutes later, when she could breathe once again. She sat up and looked at the two women who stood side by side watching her and smiling.

Angelique said, "Now you see that you can be free and experience incredible orgasms without a man. Now, if you do not mind, Tara and I need to be satisfied. Watch us and be amazed at the power of women. You can even join in if you dare."

Irene, still nude, crossed her legs and watched the scene enfold in front of her. Angelique and Tara began to kiss, their tongues exploring deep into each other's mouths. The two of them then began to explore each other's bodies. Hands caressed tits while fingers explored clits, soaking wet. A few minutes later, Tara stepped away from Angelique to put something on. Irene found herself captivated by the scene in front of her and slightly aroused. When Tara turned around again, she let out a gasp. Tara now wore a strap-on. Green in color, it was long and hard; the perfect size for the brown curls.

"Lie down," Tara told Angelique. Angelique lay down on the carpet and Irene hopped down from the table to sit on the rug beside the two women. She wanted to see the action up close. Tara spread Angelique's legs wide and knelt down between them. "Give me that lubricant over there, Irene," Tara said.

Irene gave her the lubricant and watched as she lubed the strap-on up. Then Tara knelt down between Angelique's spread thighs and slowly began to insert the strap-on with one hand. Angelique hissed and arched her back as the big, unrelenting strap-on began to slide into her. Then, suddenly, it was in and Tara gathered Angelique's ass in both hands and began to pump into her. Irene saw that Angelique was in ecstasy as her back arched with each lunge of Tara's hips and her tits shook. A few minutes later, Angelique threw back her sweaty head and let out a scream of pure animal ecstasy as her orgasm was wrenched from her.

*********

The next day, Angelique escorted Irene to a room decorated in a deep velour color of red. Plush cushions and sofas were placed all around the room. In the center of the room was a big-screened television and entertainment system. Angelique told Irene to have a seat and to make herself comfortable. Angelique walked over to the television and turned to face her. "Day three," Angelique began, "As your instructions specified, today is the day for you to see and act out a fantasy if you are brave enough to do so. There are several catches though," she added with a wide smile. "First, I want to know if it is true that one particular guest has caught your eye. My spies have informed me that you have been eyeing a certain gentleman."

Irene blushed, but said, "Your spies are correct in their assumptions. I am interested in one particular man. Stephen, I believe, is his name."

"Well," Angelique said clapping her hands, "Today is your lucky day. First, though, I need to test your level of self-pleasure. I have an array of videos for you to watch and I am going to record your arousal level. In other words, I want to be the voyeur who spies on you during your masturbation time."

Irene felt her face go hot at this statement. Angelique smiled and said, "Hey, it is okay. There is nothing to be embarrassed about."

Irene, with downcast eyes said, "You would have every right to be embarrassed if you were raised the way I was: to always be a good girl."

Angelique smiled in understanding and said, "I know your background, remember? Relax and do whatever comes naturally to you. It is okay to embrace your sexuality and freedom." With that last comment Angelique placed a DVD into the player and told Irene to have a seat on the couch. Irene did as she was told and the DVD began to play.

Irene stared in horrified fascination at the scene that began to unfold before her eyes. The woman, a big-breasted butterscotch-colored woman, laid spread eagle beneath a black and silver haired male. Her legs were wrapped around his thrusting hips, her back and neck arched. She seemed to be in ecstasy as her lover held both her hands within his as he rammed his flesh into her.

As the camera rolled in for a closer shot, Irene wet suddenly dry lips and watched as the man let go of the woman's hands to rise to his knees between her spread legs and grasp at her hips with both hands. The man wore no condom and Irene could see every wet glide of his cock as it slid in and out of the woman's butterscotch thighs. Her tightly curled black thatch glistened with moisture as his black and silver curls mashed with hers. The red flesh of her labia lovingly opened and hugged his long shaft. Half crazy with desire, the woman struggled in vain to pull her lover's head down for a kiss, but instead he pulled away and watched her with narrowed blue eyes as her full breasts shook with the force of his thrusts.

Irene had no idea when her skirt had come up as she became the woman beneath the man. The pale-yellow flowered panties she wore were scrunched between her legs, the seat of them between the lips of her vagina and the backside part scrunched tight between the cheeks of her ass. On her side, with her legs spread in a "V" and toes pointed, she arched her back, sticking her chest out. Her right hand pulled the panties tight while her left hand played with a bared breast.

Biting her bottom lip she watched the scene, breathing in short breathes. She could not believe it; the man could have been her ex-boyfriend and she the woman herself. The resemblance was uncanny, to say the least.

Irene pressed her thighs together harder, her toes pointed as she watched the scene in front of her. Suddenly the woman on the video screamed with the force of her climax. Leaning down to kiss her quickly on the lips, the man pulled away. The woman fell to her knees and opened her mouth for his still-wet cock.

Irene moaned and pinched her nipple harder as her legs suddenly stiffened; she began to cum as well. The force of her climax completely wiped her out and it took a few minutes for her to realize where she was. Her hearing gradually came back, her breathing slowed and returned to normal, and her moist eyes opened to find Angelique grinning at her.

Angelique said, "Wow, Irene, I chose the right DVD, didn't I?"

Irene straightened her clothes and said, "You sure did. I almost felt like that woman beneath my ex-boyfriend. You know, it is a shame but I never even got a chance to see what type of lover he would have been, either. I was disappointed for months for not finding that out."

Angelique said, "What happened?"

"I scared him away by trying to change him, fool that I was. I was so stupid and naïve. He had a nice long tongue too. Oops," She said with a sheepish grin, "Did I just say that?"

Angelique laughed loudly and said, "Yes, I am afraid that you did. I am glad that you felt free and were aroused enough to let yourself go. Now, though, I would like you to fulfill your ultimate fantasy of getting rid of your virginity. Are you ready?"

Irene swallowed hard and then letting out a breath and said, "Yes, I am ready to do so."

Angelique said, "Great. Stephen is waiting in the steam room. First, go into the bathroom and freshen up; then go ahead and slide into the white sarong that is waiting inside for you. Do not put any underwear on; it will make the sex easier. It will be a helluva lot sexier, too."

Irene smiled her thanks and walked into the bathroom to do as she had been told.

Stepping into the foggy, hot steam room a few minutes later, she blinked until her eyes adjusted to the dim light. She started to perspire, it seemed, immediately as the thin white sarong she had on began to cling to her otherwise naked flesh. Treading carefully on bare feet, she walked further into the room in search of her quarry. About ten feet in she stopped, startled at the sudden husky groan that came from one corner of the room. Swallowing hard in her nervousness, she straightened her shoulders and continued.

She had only walked about ten more steps when she saw him and gasped. Stephen was blindfolded and lay nude on a bench, his toffee colored flesh gleaming with steam. In front of him, on her knees, a nude blonde-haired woman was licking his burgeoning erection with pure relish. Being that his hands were bound behind him and tied beneath the bench, Stephen could only move his hips helplessly as the blonde slowly sucked his erection into her mouth, causing the husky groans to escape from his throat. Irene watched in fascination at the scene in front of her until the blonde-haired woman turned her head and saw her.

Drawing her mouth from his erection, she smiled and said, "Come on over, cherie, I was just getting him ready for you. He is almost ready. I have not let him cum because I was waiting for you."

Irene, blushing, said, "Thanks, I think," and walked towards them.

The blonde-haired woman pulled a cloth from a bag at her feet and carefully wiped Stephen's erection clean. She slipped on a white sarong like Irene's and then rose gracefully to her feet.

Stephen swore and started to get to his feet saying, "What the hell is going on here?"

The blonde, smiling at Irene, said, "Relax, love, someone else has come to take my place." Walking past Irene, she whispered in her ear, "Good luck, I know that this is your first time. Go slow, no matter what he says."

Irene whispered back her thanks and started to lift the sarong to her thighs.

She thought about removing the garment completely then decided against it and instead knotted the fabric at her waist. Stephen, still swearing, demanded to know who she was.

Where her sudden dash of courage came from, Irene would never know, but she said with pure mischief, "I am a virgin, who is about to be defiled by you; that is all you really need to know, my dear."

Stephen cursed loudly. "I do not do virgins. Untie me and let me get the hell out of here. I will finish myself off, or find another willing female, but not a virginal one to defile."

"Damn it, no," Irene said, feeling brave all of sudden. "You belong to me for now and I plan to make delicious use of your body until I get tired." After her last comment, she climbed upon his hips and, placing one hand on his chest to brace herself, reached for his erection with the other hand. Spreading her legs wide, she placed the tip of his cock between the lips of her vagina and slowly began to sink down on it. He felt strange between her small tender opening and a helluva lot bigger then her gynecologist doctor's finger ever had.

As soon as his erection slid between her legs, Stephen's hips lifted up. No longer swearing, he muttered, "Damn it, place your hands on my chest and ride me. I need to cum so bad. If you untie my hands, I will even guide you if you want me to do so, my bold little soon-to-be no-longer virgin."

Blushing, even though he could not see her, Irene said, "Okay, I think that I do need some help, but you have to promise not to remove your blindfold."

Stephen paused for half a second then said, "I promise not to remove the blindfold."

Climbing down from his hips, Irene reached under the bench and untied his hands. As soon as she did, Stephen reached for her, saying, "Climb back up; I need to cum now." Feeling the sarong, he said, "Take off your clothes too, I want to feel your nipples."

Irene removed her sarong as he asked, climbed back up on his hips and spread her legs.

Gasping her hips in his hands, he brought her body down as his hips rose up to meet hers. Irene gasped and tried to pull away from his grip. The pain was unexpected and excruciating.

Yet he resisted her frantic struggles. "Relax; Stop fighting me, my brave little virgin. I will make it better for you. Breathe, just breathe for a minute," he muttered with his face in a grimace.

Irene struggled to do as he asked. She sat, inhaling and exhaling as she felt his foreign erection foreign pulsating between her tender tissues. "Okay," she said at last. "I am ready, I think."

Stephen said, "About damn time," as he painfully gripped her hips. "Now ride me like you would ride a horse. Let your body follow the motions of my hips."

Irene slowly began to move up and down, then in a circle, her body swaying to a dance of its own making.

Stephen, groaning, removed one hand from her hip and worked two fingers into her nest of curls to rub at that super sensitive nub of flesh.

Irene moaned, eyes closed, and leaning back on her huaraches, arched her back. He felt so good, his fingers were positively wicked. Gripping at her breasts with her hands, she pulled at her distended nipples.

Stephen gripped her hips harder with his hands, then leaned up to say, "Remove your hands, I want to taste you."

Irene gasped and opened her eyes to say, "You lied."

"I never said that I was a saint," Stephen said with half a smile, his green eyes staring deep into her wide dark-brown ones. Then still joined with her body, he rolled her over onto her back and leaned down to take a bite at one of her nipples. His hands gripped hers as he slammed them down by her head. He spread her legs wider and plunged deeper inside of her.    Irene started to moan, he felt so good with his hardness pressing into her softness. She had just started to close her eyes once again, when Stephen said, "No, look at me. Keep your eyes on mine. I want you to watch me when I cum because I am going to watch you when you cum."

Irene's world began to tilt out of control moments later as her legs curled around his sweaty back, her feet pressed into his thrusting buttocks. Arching her neck, she screamed as the sensations became too much for her to bear. Her last thought before she began to climax was that she was going to have a ton of bruises tomorrow.

Biting her bottom lip, her eyes watery, she watched Stephen as he swore and picked up speed, his hips thrusting faster. A few seconds later, his powerful body jerked upon hers and he began to climax, too. His green eyes were squinting, but still staring unwaveringly into hers, the entire time he came. She felt him shoot his load into her inner cavity with a sense of wonder.

Minutes later, they lay together, his head in her hair, his body still joined with hers, as his hand roamed almost absentmindedly across her breasts. Completely relaxed, he muttered sleepily, "You know, I do not even know your name."

Smoothing her hands across his sweaty back, she said, "Irene."

Stephen lifted his head and said with a grin, his green eyes twinkling, "Glad to meet you, Irene. My name is Stephen. Now if you don't mind, I must get up or else I am afraid that I may turn into a steamed mushroom."

Irene laughed and said, "I would certainly not want that either. I have to go, too."

Stephen drew back and she tried to stop her gasp of pain, but he heard it anyway. He stood fully, grabbed a pair of shorts nearby, and stepped into them.

With genuine concern in his eyes, Stephen said, "Go back to your room and take a hot bath, it will ease the pain. I only know this because I defiled my high school girlfriend and she told me how she stopped the pain. You were my second virgin, Irene," he said grinning. He laughed at her blush and tossed the sarong at her. Turning towards the door, he paused at the exit and said, "I will see you around."

Irene had her head down and was wrapping the sarong around her as she thought to herself, "That was just great. That man made the most incredible love to me and then vanishes right before my eyes."

Walking somewhat stiffly, she made her way back to her hotel room and stepped into the bathroom. She had stripped and was running the water in the tub when she noticed a box of treats. Opening the box, she found bubble bath, peppermint massage oil, chocolates, a special jelly for her tender tissues, strawberries, apple cider and plenty of fluffy still warm towels. Angelique had attached a note, as well, stating that she hoped that all had gone well and that she would see her at dinner if Irene felt up to it. Angelique also instructed Irene to press play on the remote for the stereo.

Irene pressed play on the remote and smiled with delight as Enya's haunting voice filled the room. She stepped into the tub and, as she sunk beneath the golden bubbles, she reminded herself to thank Angelique for her thoughtfulness.

********

The next morning, when Angelique knocked on Irene's door at eight a.m., Irene had been up and dressed for an hour already.

"Wow!" Angelique said, "You are up early. How was last night?"

Irene, dressed in a bright yellow sundress and sandals, grinned widely at her. "I had a wonderful time actually; I never knew how good it could be. I am wondering to myself why the hell I waited so long to give it up. But what is even more amazing is that I feel no aches and pains. I guess the jelly really did its job. I did notice a slight bruising on my hips and buttocks though. Still... I feel no real pain."

Angelique laughed loudly, then handed her the usual blue sealed envelope saying, "I hope that you enjoy today's activity as well. Come on down to the dining room if you are hungry. I have to go right now, but I will be back a little while later."

Irene exclaimed, "I am too excited to eat. I cannot wait to see what today's naughty activity involves!"

The door shut behind Angelique and Irene carefully slit open the envelope. The card inside read the following: "Day Four- Character/Role Play Day—You have been chosen to play a famous character from history, the role of Lady Godiva. Go to the stables immediately for further details and instructions. This escapade may end up being your most exciting one yet."

Upon reaching the stables she was led to a bareback thoroughbred horse. Looking at the guy from the stables who led her to the horse, she said, "I have never ridden bareback before, I am not sure about this."

"Irene, you will be fine," he assured her. "Besides, you will not be riding alone."

"Whatever do you mean? Lady Godiva, if I remember my history correctly, rode naked alone."

"This is true," he continued on to say, "But today you will not be riding alone. Plus, after having read your folder, you will need only to strip down to your underwear. Ah, here is your gentleman escort right now. Irene, please meet Robert. Robert, meet Irene."

Irene turned around and looked up into the dark chocolate-brown gaze of Robert's.

Robert was too gorgeous for words. Standing about six feet tall, he had black curls that fell in slight disarray around his shoulders. He was barefoot and dressed in a white pair of flowing slacks. His bronze hair-covered chest was slightly sheen with sweat. He looked liked a Latin lover from a romance cover. Grinning widely at her, he said, "So, nice to finally meet you, Irene. Stephen has told me about you."

Irene could not help herself, she blushed immediately as Robert mentioned Stephen's name. Robert let out a small chuckle at her reaction, his dark eyes curving wickedly. "There is no reason to be embarrassed, Irene. Stephen mentioned only great things about you my dear," Robert said with a smile. "Follow me, please, and I can show you where you can strip down."

Slightly nervous, yet excited beyond words, Irene turned to follow him into a small room not too far from the stables. Robert opened the door for her and took a step back so that she could walk through before him.

Irene walked into the room and then turned towards him, expectantly.

"Do I have permission to stay, love? Or would you prefer to disrobe in private?" he asked, throwing a wide smile at her.

Her top teeth worried at her bottom lip for a minute, and then she said in a small voice, "Yes, you can stay, but please turn your back for now."

"Delighted!" he said and walked further into the room as the door snapped shut behind him.

Irene turned her back to him and then stripped out of her sundress, leaving her bra and panties on. She turned back towards him and watched as his dark eyes ran down the length of her body.

"Nice. I especially like your chest," he said with a smile. "The stilettos are nice too, although not quite appropriate for ridding, I am afraid."

Irene felt her face go hot, but she smiled back at him. "I am afraid that I could not quite part with my bra and panties just yet. I..."

Robert interrupted her and said, "I will take care of it, stop worrying. You are still not completely comfortable yet about all of this, but before this morning is over you will be, trust me. I don't bite, love, not unless provoked or asked." He ended the last comment with a laugh, than held out his right hand to her.

Irene walked towards him and took the hand that he offered her. Robert opened the door and the two of them walked out into the sunshine to a waiting brown thoroughbred mare. Robert released her hand and quickly swung himself up onto the mare's back then held a hand out to Irene. Irene placed her hand in his and then barely swallowed her gasp of disbelief when he easily lifted and placed her in front of him on the horse.

Robert pulled her close, back into his arms, and then whispered in her ear, "Relax, it is okay. Place a hand on each one of my thighs."

Irene complied with his request and slowly let her head fall back to rest against the curve of his neck.

"Okay?" his lips breathed the word at her temple.

"Okay," Irene said.

Robert put the horse into motion and the two of them set off, heading towards one of the many secluded paths that ran the length of the property. Irene began to relax after they had been riding for about five minutes.

The scenery was beautiful, the heavy scent of rain from the early morning thunderstorm hung in the area. There was no breeze, though, and after a while Irene begin to sweat. A trickle of her sweat trailed down from her neck to land in the valley between her breasts. When the second trickle of sweat started to drift down her onto her chest, she removed a hand from Robert's thigh to wipe at it. Robert gasped her wrist with one of his hands even before her hand could make contact with her moist skin.

"Irene," he said, smiling down at her when she turned her head around to look at him. "Let me take care of that." He coaxed the horse to a stop, then, holding her eyes with his the entire time; he smoothed his hands across her stomach and slowly moved them up to her chest. When his hands reached her red bra, he moved one strap down her shoulder, and then afforded the other strap the same treatment. Both of his hands reached up to cup a breast in each hand as Irene hissed in a breath. Her nipples puckered the thin fabric at the first clasp of his huge warm hands.

"Irene, my sweet, I love this bra, I really do; But may I take it off?" Robert asked.

Still staring into his eyes, but unable to speak, Irene nodded her head, giving him her consent.

Robert smiled at her and then reached his hands around to the clasp behind her back. The bra slid into his waiting hands and he tossed it to the ground. Irene started to protest, but he hushed her, placing one finger against her lips.

"I will take care of you. You don't need your bra anymore," he said, cupping her chin with his hand and placing a gentle kiss on top of her forehead. "Turn around and straddle my thighs."

Turning around carefully, with him helping her the whole time, Irene did as he asked. Robert smiled at her for a minute, his hands clasping her waist, before his eyes fell to her full breasts. Irene sucked in her breath when, a second later, he leaned down to trail his tongue down the same path that the trickle of sweat had taken. Her stomach caving in, she leaned back onto the horse's back, moaning. His long hair tickled at her sensitive flesh, as he licked at her warm sun-kissed skin. Cupping her shoulders in his hands, he pulled her up to meet his mouth. Turning his head, he licked at each of her pointed nipples.

Moaning, Irene arched her back and reaching up she tangled her fingers in his long hair to hold him against her chest. Robert laved her nipples a few more minutes, his teeth gently nipping at them before he raised his head from her hot, wet flesh.

Untangling her fingers from out of his hair, Robert smiled down at her when her eyes popped opened. She started to mutter a protest, blinking in confusion, but he reassured her.

"Hey, it's okay, cupcake. You are so responsive; I cannot wait to come inside you. I want to get between those beautiful thighs. Sit up and unwrap your legs from around me so that I can take these pants off. I am about to burst, but I want to burst inside of you. I want to be inside of you when I cum. Are you going to let me remove those sexy little panties too? Let me remove my pants then I can take them off too as well."

Irene did as he asked and Robert slid down, off of the horse's back. Brushing the horse's mane with his hand, Robert instructed the mare to stay still, then removed his pants. After removing his pants, Robert reached up and removed her tiny red panties. Irene let out a gasp when he climbed back onto the mare's back and faced her once again. Gathering her close to him, Robert said, "You can wrap those legs back around me now."

Licking her lips, Irene wrapped her arms around his shoulders and wrapped her legs back around his waist. The tip of Robert's pulsing, hot cock teased at her dark brown curls for a minute before Robert reached down and cupped her ass with both hands. When he breached her curls and pushed into her, Irene gasped, feeling her sensitive tissues stretching to let him inside.

Leaning down to kiss her ear, Robert whispered, "You are so tight, I love it! Don't be alarmed, but I am about to start the horse moving now. Just a slow trot, I will hold onto you, so don't worry about falling. Move with the motion of the horse or do whatever movement feels natural to you."

Robert started the mare off to a slow trot with his legs and then squeezed the cheeks of her ass with both hands. Face pressed against his hard shoulder, Irene gasped, feeling his cock spear up into her nether regions. Robert's hips slammed into her trembling, quivering body, his cock kissing her tiny nub of flesh over and over again. Involuntarily, Irene felt her hips moving with the mare's movements, moving up to meet Roberts' hard thrusts. She sank her teeth into his shoulder blade as the sensations became too much all of a sudden. Letting out a scream, her eyes fell closed as she came.

"Fuck!" Robert exclaimed as he felt the sharp edge of her teeth sink into his taut flesh. "Little tiger. Okay, cupcake, I am going to give you what you need."

He suddenly stopped the horse. Irene's eyes popped open in surprise when she felt the mare stop.

"What... what's going?" Irene asked, licking her parched lips, lifting her head from off of his shoulder.

"Nothing yet, cupcake," Robert said, giving her a strained smile, "But something will happen soon."

Irene looked at him in confusion when he kneed the mare to a stop and pulled completely out of her. Still hard, his cock shiny and wet with her juices, Robert slid off of the horse's back and pulled a still-confused Irene down to stand beside him.

Linking their hands together, Robert pulled her with him towards one of the nearby cabanas that had been set up on the sandy beach. Once inside, he urged her to lie down on the bed inside and came down on top of her. His hard legs slid in between her spread ones. Rising to his knees, he stuck his swollen cock back into her. Irene reached up to grab the headboard with both hands as he began to move inside of her, her back arching up off the bed. Leaning over her, Robert covered her hands with his then suddenly shoved deeper inside of her and began to cum. Irene felt him shoot his load into her inner cavity, the cum warm from his body. Collapsing on top of her body a few moments later, Robert leaned down and kissed her softly on the lips.

Kissing her neck, he whispered against her right ear, "Incredible, just incredible... all of that sweet tightness milking me." Clasping her waist, he flipped her over to lie on top of him, her head tucked under his chin.

Irene sleepily muttered a contented 'hmmm', than placed one hand on his chest and the other on his shoulder as she closed her eyes. The two of them fell asleep on one accord, exhausted from their activity.

An hour later, Irene and Robert awoke and dressed in the white sheer togas that they found in a nearby chest. Robert helped Irene climb back onto the mare's back and the two of them began their trek back towards the compound. They had been riding for about ten minutes or so when they heard a noise in a nearby patch of woods. Slowing the horse to a stop, Robert slid down off of its back and gently guided it along with one hand to a slow walk. Irene had started to protest when he slid from the horse's back, but he pressed a finger to his lips. Squeezing Irene's thigh gently, his dark eyes urged her to be silent. She complied with his command and the two of them resumed their quest to get closer to the source of the noise. A few seconds later, Irene barely suppressed a gasp at the sight that greeted her eyes, when she saw where the noise had come from.

Robert turned towards her and whispered, "Hush, its okay. Come on slide down here beside me."

He helped her off the mare's back and urged her to stand in front of him, wrapping his arms around her waist. The two of them stood and watched the scene unfold in front of them. Three naked men, one blond-haired man, one dark-haired man and one black man were lost in an orgy fest. Their bodies were a contrast of color; two deeply bronzed the other darker in color to his counterparts. Irene recognized the blond to be Andrew. The other two males she recognized to be Carroll and Ryan.

Andrew laid spread eagle on a blanket, while Ryan, on all fours, sucked his cock. Carroll was behind Ryan, knees slightly bent, driving his cock deep into Ryan's ass. Andrew's back arched, head thrown back as he groaned aloud with ecstasy. His fingers shoved deep into Ryan's dark hair. Ryan's open mouth slid up and down Andrew's long shaft as Carroll fucked his ass. Carroll's hands gripped Ryan's hips and occasionally fondled and pinched the cheeks of his ass.

Irene had never seen or experienced anything like this before, yet found herself completely enthralled at the sight before her. She leaned back into Robert's embrace, her hands gripping at Robert's forearms, her breathing deepening, her heart racing in excitement. She felt Robert chuckle softly in her. Then she felt his hands go to the ties that held her toga together. His fingers made quick work of the ties and the toga fell to the ground to puddle at her feet. Irene's hands fell to gasp his hard thighs as one of his hands cupped one of her tits, while the other one trailed down the swell of her stomach to delve between her curls.

Irene hissed in her breath and spread her legs to accommodate Robert's questing fingers. Arching her back slightly, she watched the scene play out in front of her, trembling. Robert shoved two fingers deep inside of her, while another one of his fingers pinched at her swollen nipple.

Irene watched as Andrew gripped Ryan's dark head harder all of a sudden and began to cum, his hips arching up off of the blanket. Carroll leaned over Ryan's back, hips jerking and started to cum inside his ass. The two men groaned loudly and Irene just couldn't help herself, she screamed aloud just then.

Robert's hand came up to cover her mouth but it had not been fast enough; the three men had heard her. Carroll, now standing and in the process of cleaning his flaccid cock with a wet cloth, turned towards the woods. Ryan, still on his knees and sipping a bottle of water, turned around while Andrew rose up off of the blanket on his elbows in search of the noise. Robert calmly pulled his other hand away from the juices between her trembling thighs and casually licked his fingers clean. Between licks, he said, "Now you have done it, cupcake. They know that we are here and they know that we watched them the whole entire time. We might as well go ahead and show our faces now."

Irene, mortified beyond belief, licked her lips and whispered, "Oh, no!"

She started to reach for her toga to cover her naked form, but Robert shook his head at her.

Holding his hand out to her, he said, "It's a little too late for that. Come on, we might as well go say hello to them. Besides, you saw them naked, now it is only fair that they see you as well."

Irene knew that he was right, so she placed her small, cool hand in his and the two of them walked out of the patch of woods into the clearing. Far from being embarrassed, the three men burst out laughing when they saw the two of them.

"Did you guys enjoy the show?" Carroll asked tossing the cloth into a nearby trash can.

Robert grinned widely and said, "I think that our little Irene here enjoyed the show more than I did. I am not really into that man on man thing, but it really turned Cupcake on. She came undone in my arms watching you guys. I tried to cover her mouth but didn't end up doing it fast enough."

Irene felt her face grow warm at the last statement that Robert made.

Ryan rose to his feet, laughing, and said, "Why don't we make her pay for being so wanton?"

Andrew said, "That's an excellent idea, besides I would love to see our dear sweet Irene lose control once again. What do you think about that, Irene? Hmm...?" Andrew rose up off of the blanket and extended his hand out to her then. Smiling at her, he said, "Come here, cupcake, don't be shy. We only want to satisfy your every need, your every desire."

Irene hesitated for half of a second; Andrew could not possibly be suggesting...

Understanding her inner dilemma, Robert rubbed her back soothingly and said, "It is okay, Irene, we only want to pleasure you. You are full of such passion."

A few seconds later, Irene walked towards Andrew, holding his blue gaze the whole entire time.

Andrew pulled her down onto the blanket beside him so that she ended up flat on her back. Leaning over Irene, he placed a kiss upon her forehead, then leaned back and motioned Ryan over to them. Andrew moved behind her and placed Irene's head in his lap. Stroking her hair and face with his hands, Andrew smiled down at her for a minute, then leaned over and pressed a brief kiss to her mouth. Ryan came over to them, got on his knees between Irene's legs and spread her thighs apart with his hands. Ryan's hard cock speared through her thatch of curls and, cupping her butt in both hands, he reared up into her. He drove deep inside of her, his long, thick cock plowing her aching walls.

Irene arched up, her mouth falling open to scream at his first hard thrust, but her scream was cut off as her mouth was quickly covered with Andrew's. Andrew nipped at her bottom lip then slid his tongue inside.

Irene opened her eyes when she felt hands cupping her tits, plucking at the nipples, then two tongues licking and sucking at the hard, pointed tips. Carroll and Robert had joined her and Andrew on the blanket and were making a feast of her tits. Each of Irene's hands came up to clasp Carroll and Robert's heads to her swollen flesh, then her eyes fell closed once again.

Lost in a passion-filled haze, she began to see various colors of the rainbow float before her closed eyelids as her breath came faster. Ryan thrust harder into her, his cock irritating the little nub between her thighs as Irene wrapped her legs tighter around his pumping hips. About a minute later, it all became too much for her; Irene came once, twice, three times. Irene shook and shuddered as her muscles clamped down on Ryan's cock. Irene's juices flowed out of her to drench Ryan's cock and, pulling her head from out of Andrew's clasp, she screamed loud. Before blacking out, she vaguely felt Ryan's warm cum shoot into her inner cavity.

Irene came to a few minutes later to find Robert kneeling on his knees, rubbing a wet cloth between her thighs.

She looked around and said, "Where did everyone go?"

Robert laughed and said, "Their job was done, they all left. You are something else." He said the last remark smiling down at her while he finished cleaning her sensitive tissues.

A minute later he slid down between her legs and began to eat her out. Using his fingers, he speared her thatch open and licked the top of her clitoris, then licked down the sides. Irene's hips titled up, her hands sliding down into Robert's long strands. Robert grasped her butt into both of his hands as his tongue swirled around her tiny nub of flesh and sucked it between his lips. A few minutes later she came, shuddering, her juices flowing into his mouth. Robert pulled her hands out of his hair, helped her stand up and redressed her once more into the toga.

"Come on," he said. "Let's go. Poor cupcake, you must be exhausted from all of your activities. You can ride side saddle-back; I know you must be sore."

Kissing her on the forehead he helped her get on the horse and the two of them headed back to the resort. Thirty minutes later, when the two of them arrived back at the resort, Robert returned the horse to the stables then swept her up in his arms to carry her inside.

Angelique met them inside. She instructed Robert to carry Irene to her room. Robert carried Irene, not only to her hotel room, but into the bathroom where he proceeded to tend to her. He sat her on the edge of the tub, filling it with soothing warm water.

Once the door of the suite had shut behind Robert, Angelique turned towards Irene with a wide grin and said, "So I heard that you had a really exciting time today. Andrew told me all about it."

Irene felt her face go hot, but she said, "Yes I had a great time. I mean it seemed almost surreal, to have all of that attention focused on little ole me."

Angelique laughed and said, "Don't be so embarrassed, Irene. This is what you came here for: to experience things, to be free. Hop into the tub while I order room service for you, you must be famished. Take a nap if you want and join me for dinner later if you are up to it."

Irene did as she was told and eased her tired body into the warm bubbles. An hour later, after eating the chicken salad and fresh fruit, Irene tumbled into bed.

*******

The next morning, Angelique walked into the suite and handed her another blue envelope and said, "Today is your last day Irene, I hope that this has been both a very rewarding and enlightening experience for you. It has been a real joy to know you and I hope that you return once again to enjoy our services in the future."

Pausing at the door, she turned back around to say, "You know Irene, some of our clients have been known to hook up after leaving here. Perhaps you will be so lucky. Either Stephen and Robert would be quite the catch."

Angelique smiled at the shocked expression on Irene's face and walked out the door.

Irene opened the envelope to read the small card enclosed inside.

"Day Five- What are cookies without the cream? Today's activity is guaranteed to make you scream! Pleasures abound. Go to the indoor pool area immediately! Put on your best looking swimsuit, or don't put a swimsuit on at all!"

Irene laughed aloud and quickly brushed her teeth and showered. She was definitely in a hurry to see what was in store for today.

Thirty minutes later, dressed in a light blue swimsuit, on bare feet, she walked into the pool area to find Robert and Stephen waiting for her. Smiling at them, she said "Hello, didn't expect to see both of you guys here!"

Dressed in blue swim trunks, they laughed, and Stephen said, "Robert has been telling me all about your activities. It sounds like you have really been having a great time. Come on, Robert and I want to show you something."

Irene took his outstretched hand and Stephen guided her to the shallow part of the pool; Robert trailed along behind them. Robert stepped into the pool and, still holding her hand, Irene and Stephen joined them. Stephen sat down on a ledge in the pool and pulled Irene in front of him, so that she stood between his spread thighs. Wrapping one arm around her waist, he cupped her chin with the other and began to kiss her.

Irene laid her head on his shoulder and kissed him back, her hands sliding down to reach inside his trunks to cup his bare butt. Her hands squeezed the cheeks of his ass as Stephen slid his tongue deep inside of her mouth, her nipples hardening into tiny points as she felt his erection press against her stomach. Stephen lifted his head a few minutes later, just when she started to get light-headed, and pushed her away from him a few feet.

Irene, confused, started to protest, until she felt Robert press a kiss to her ear and say, "Shhh, cupcake, it is okay, we are going to take care of you. Relax and enjoy."

She sucked in a breath when she realized that he had removed the blue swimming trunks. Robert's hard erection pressed against her butt, between her ass cheeks, through the crease of the swimsuit.

Stephen reached down into the water and removed his swimming trunks then, looking at Robert, said, "Help her out of her suit, man; I want to touch those big tits once again."

Holding Stephen's green gaze with her dark-brown, Irene stood still as Robert undressed her in front of him. Once she was naked, Stephen reached out a hand and pulled her back towards him. Cupping her ass cheeks in both hands, Robert pressed his body against her back and gently pushed her towards Stephen. Once she reached Stephen, to stand once more between his spread thighs, he lifted one of her tits out of the water and licked at the hard nipple.

Irene's eyes fell slightly closed and she let out a moan, her head falling back against Robert's hard shoulder. Stephen licked both of her nipples, and then lifted his head to look into her passion filled gaze. Cupping her chin with both hands, he said, "Robert and I want to have you at the same time, to experience you at the same time. We want to cum inside your beautiful body deep and feel your muscles clenching our cocks. Do you trust enough to let us do that, cupcake? Hmm? You don't have to say anything, just nod your head if you will allow us the pleasure."

Irene chewed her bottom lip for a second, and then she slowly nodded her consent. Stephen scooted to the edge of the ledge and wrapped her thighs around his waist. Stephen's cock slid in between her wet folds and pushed inside of her, but he didn't thrust up into her. Stephen slid his hands into her hair and began to kiss her once more, while Robert slid his fingers along the crease of her ass cheeks. Irene knew then what they were going to do and her body trembled slightly, her heart beating in anticipation. She was about to be taken from the front as well as from behind, and for some strange reason this excited her beyond belief. Robert's fingers made a place for his cock just then and Irene sucked in a breath. Robert's cock was long and hard and the hole of her anus was small. It hurt a bit and her muscles protested. Stephen's mouth swallowed her cry of pain, than suddenly Robert was inside of her virginal anus cavity. Robert placed a kiss onto her ear and said, "Cupcake you are so sweet, tight. I love the feel of being in your ass." He placed his hands on the sides of the pool behind Stephen and said, "I am ready, man. Take her."

Stephen wrapped both arms around Robert's back and reared up into Irene's pussy, his cock thrusting deep. Robert, in return, plowed his way into her anus. Irene pulled her mouth from Stephen's and screamed, arching her back. Irene had never experienced anything like this before in her life. She kissed Stephen as her body was anchored by two hard male bodies; she could do nothing as they began to thrust up into her.

Robert's hard chest pressed against her back as Stephen's chest pressed against her hard nipples. Back and forth her hips swirled: her pussy forward to ride Stephen's cock, her ass backwards to ride Robert's cock. The water lapped over their bodies as the three of them picked up speed and a few seconds later, Irene came.

Body shuddering, Irene sank her teeth into the side of Stephen's neck. Stephen sucked in a breath, his hands pulled at her hair as his hips pushed up inside of her. A few seconds later he came, shooting his warm cum inside of her inner cavity, causing Irene to cum once more. Robert's warm cum filled her anus a second later and Irene's body went slack.

Robert chuckled in her ear, and then kissed the top of her head. He pulled away from her body and climbed out of the pool.

Irene sagged into Stephen's arms, wrapping her arms around his neck and kissed him softly on the lips. Robert dressed once again in swimming trunks said to Stephen, "Take care of her, man. That sexy little thing is a keeper."

Stephen said, "I will, man, thanks. She is awesome." Sweeping her up in his arms, he stepped out of the pool and took her into one of the huge shower rooms.

As Stephen stood Irene on her feet, she looked up at him and asked, "Stephen, does this mean that I belong to you now?"

Stephen laughed and said, "Baby you belonged to me the moment I took your virginity from you. However, I need to know if you want me, too?"

Irene smiled at him and said, "Yes, I do indeed. From the moment I saw you on the plane, that is. But, Stephen, I like Robert too as well."

Stephen said, "Hmm...you do? Well, I have never been that good at sharing, but we will see..."

# **_Engagement of Congress Contract_**

The purpose of this document is to acquire the services
of _____ on _____ 2007, (who will be
referred to as the Audacious Apprentice for the duration
of this contract) to engage in the most forbidden, but
oh so delicious, activities ever imagined by any homo-
sapiens. Sexual relations with_____ on
_____ 2007, (who will be referred to as the
Mistress of Relations for the duration of this contract)
will exceed all of my earthly desires and beyond.

I acknowledge that, although quite horny, I am in my
right frame of mind. I expect to be used over and over
again as the Mistress of Relations instructs me in sexual
relations. I expect to be tied, spanked lightly,
blindfolded, and tickled with a feather if the Mistress of
Relations insists upon it henceforth. I will fully comply
with the Mistress of Relations if she so requests me to
kiss, lick, eat, suck toes or any other part of her
voluptuous body. I, the Audacious Apprentice will try
not to disappoint the Mistress of Relations and will give
her all of the orgasms that she can withstand.

I, the Audacious Apprentice, in return for my services
will not be humiliated with cruel words or insults. I will
also not be whipped, made to bleed or defecated upon
by the Mistress of Relations at any time during the
duration of this contract. I understand the Mistress of
Relations desire for discretion so not a word of this shall
be discussed the next time I hang out with my male
friends.

In addition, if the Mistress of Relations announces that her hunger lingers beyond the above date, I, (the ever horny Audacious Apprentice) will be more then willing to extend my learning, indefinitely.

Before beginning this most naughty but informative task, I, the (Audacious Apprentice) will purchase a mega box of condoms and lubricant from the local drugstore. These items, essential to enhance both the security and pleasure of both parties involved, will be used accordingly. In addition, in an attempt to make a really good first impression on the Mistress of Relations, I will treat her to a lovely dinner at an Italian restaurant followed by a box of scrumptious chocolates.

Kissed & Signed by the two overly eager individuals listed above_____&_____on _____2007.

Audacious Apprentice

Mistress of Relations

*Notes: The Mistress of Relations will not be held responsible for any minor bites or scratches that the Audacious Apprentice may receive during the course of this engagement. This legal, binding contract can only be terminated by the two parties listed above, not by any other hypocritical or judgmental male or female.

Skye Ryan is a pseudonym for a 30 year old Pisces female. Gainfully employed; she works two jobs and spins tales in her spare time. She enjoys the English language and has a general love affair with words.

Ms. Ryan resides in Maryland, she can be reached via e-mail at skyeryan35@yahoo.com. She can also be found on Myspace.com at the following link: http://www.myspace.com/skyeryan35. In addition, you can write to Ms. Ryan at P.O. Box 693, Princess Anne, Maryland 21853.